# New Beginnings

Other Books by

Lynette Snell

Tainted Love




Soon to be released

Hidden Truths

# *New Beginnings*

by

## Lynette Snell

For Mark

The love of my life

Thank you to everyone who helped me get this book to print and for my family for their never ending stream of support.

# Chapter One

Waterlogged debris lay scattered along the length of the shoreline. A vivid reminder of the overnight storm that had battered the coast of Maine. A lone figure stood amongst the rocks that formed a barrier between the encroaching tide and the low coastal lands that stretched out behind her. Their images were slowly fading. She had lain in her bed listening to the sound of the storm in all its fury, knowing only too well the power of its wrath. If only she had had the chance to look on their faces one last time and say goodbye. A long sigh escaped her lips. Two years had passed and the guilt still weighed heavily on her mind. She had hoped that coming home would help her recapture a time in her life when she had truly felt happy. Her eyes moistened. She had lost her virginity to Alistair out here under a blanket of stars and to the soothing sound of the breaking waves.

She gave a startled gasp as the chilly spring tide crept up and lapped around her ankles. Hurriedly she gathered her long dress up into her arms, its hem now heavy with water. Another wave crashed over the rocks knocking her off balance. A piercing scream punctured the air, as she toppled into the churning water below. When she  finally broke the surface there was only just enough time for her to manage a quick gasp of air before she was dragged below the waves. Her long dress wrapped around her legs as she made a desperate bid for the surface. As daylight appeared, she snatched another quick gulp of air just as another wave crashed over her head. She coughed up a mouthful of water. The tide tossed her around, bringing her within arm's length of the rocks then teasingly drawing her away. It was obvious that she was no match against the power of the sea. Her eyes desperately scanned the shoreline. Everywhere she looked, waves ruthlessly crashed against the rocks. Spying a low lying outcrop of rocks she made a last ditch effort toward them. The going was painfully slow as each time she felt she was succeeding, the tide would draw her back out. By the time she reached them she was exhausted and the chill of the early spring water had begun to take its toll. Ditching the dress would be the smart thing to do, but it had been Alistair's favourite. She knew it was stupid to be sentimental about a silly dress, especially when her life was in danger, but she couldn't bring herself to rid herself of it. Her limbs felt heavy and every breath she took felt as if there was a tight bandage wrapped around her chest preventing her lungs from filling. The combination of the churning sea and the constant drag of the water laden dress was making it almost impossible to keep her head above water. Her fingers and toes were numb with cold and her lips had lost their pink healthy glow. With the little strength she had left, she reached out and grabbed hold of the rocks and pulled herself up out of the water. Just when she thought she had made it her dress snagged on the rocks below. Plastered against the rock gripping tightly with one hand she used the other to try and free it. In her weakened state she couldn't find the strength to tear it. Defeated she slipped back into the water. She clung limply to the rock her energy now almost completely depleted. Another wave crashed over her head. Thoughts of her husband and son drifted to the forefront of her mind. Was this how they had spent the last moments of their precious lives? Struggling to breathe as the ocean slowly sucked the life out of them. Their frightened faces floated before her; she wanted so much to be with them. Slowly she exhaled and let herself drop below the surface. Did she even want to live? A peaceful calm settled over her. Her daughter's happy little face suddenly appeared before her. With screaming lungs she headed for the surface. How could she have even considered abandoning her daughter? She tore at one of the shoulder straps of her dress and felt it give way.

She reached across onto her other shoulder. A startled gasp escaped her lips when a hand clamped around her upper arm and she was suddenly hauled from the water. She had a vague awareness of being carried across the rocks to the safety of the beach. The next thing she knew, she was lying flat on her back on the sand staring up at the clear blue sky. It took a minute or two for her brain to process what had happened. She pushed herself up into a sitting position. Her chest rose and fell as she fought to regain her breath. Her eyes settled on a pair of bronzed feet and muscular calves. Feeling at a sudden disadvantage, she tried to rise to her feet. Her foot caught in the torn hem of her dress and she lurched forward. He caught her against his bare chest. Giving an impatient grunt he pushed her away, ensuring to keep a firm grip on her arm until she had regained her balance. Her eyes slowly travelled up the length of his body, taking in the trim toned abdomen, slim waist and muscular chest, followed by a set of broad shoulders. A small gasp escaped her lips when her eyes reached his face. Heat flooded to her cheeks. He looked back at her in cold silence, his eyes showing no sign of compassion. Unnerved by the intensity of his stare, she took a quick step backwards. A shiver ran up her spine, as he stood there boldly assessing her, with what could only be described as impatient irritation. Her eyes scanned the bay deliberately avoiding his gaze. Nervously twisting her dress in her hands she dared another quick glance at him. He smiled, causing another pink flush to flood her cheeks. It was hard not to notice the dramatic change to his appearance. Soft laughter lines appeared around his eyes and mouth. An unexpected warmth showed in his eyes.

She moved her focus to her hands, hoping he would say something, instead of just standing there openly staring at her. He had to admit, she was attractive in a wet, bedraggled sort of way and the blushing, he found rather amusing. Her deep emerald green eyes momentarily met his, and something primal stirred inside him. The barriers instantly went up. "What the hell did you think you were doing?"

A shiver ran up her spine at the venom in his voice. "I, I... slipped," she replied, nervously pushing her hair back off her face in a futile attempt to correct her dishevelled appearance. His eyes were instantly drawn to where the shoulder strap of her dress had been torn away, exposing a delicious piece of creamy white flesh. Every movement she made caused the dress to shift slightly. His eyes eagerly skimmed across her exposed flesh taking in the full rounded crest of her breast. His body went rigid. He didn't particularly like the thoughts that were now running through his head. It wasn't often he had this reaction to a woman, especially not one he had only just met. She looked up giving him a hint of a smile, her long dark lashes fluttering across her beautiful green eyes. He clenched his fists, what was he thinking? In his experience women only ever wanted one thing, his money. Why would this one be any different? Well, he wasn't about to fall for the old 'damsel in distress' routine. He fixed her with one of his frosty stares "slipped..., an unlikely story," he said curtly.

Her eyes narrowed "Excuse me!"

"You heard me."

She placed her hands on her hips, her teeth gave a little chatter. "You think I..." The thought of how close she had actually come to giving up made her hesitate.

He shrugged, "Oh come on..., let's be honest here."

She glared at him unable to form any words

He gave an exasperated sigh, "Why don't you just admit it, you threw yourself off the rocks..."

Her mouth dropped open. He gave her a smug grin, "I'm right aren't I?"

Her eyes widened as he punched at the air with his fist. "I knew it. I've been watching you for weeks, standing out there all alone, staring out at the ocean. It was only a matter of time"

Her temper flared, "And that's the only possible conclusion you could come up with?"

He smiled, "Pretty much."

Her fists bunched in the water laden fabric of her dress. "How dare you say such a thing. You don't even know me."

His eyes darkened, causing another cold shiver to run up her spine, "And I'd like to keep it that way."

She squared her shoulders, fixing him with a stare that clearly told him he had overstepped the mark. "Well you won't have to worry on that score because the feelings mutual."

"At least we agree on something" he replied gruffly.

She glowered at him "You're despicable, you know that."

He grinned "So I've been told."

She gave a frustrated groan, "So why did you even bother coming to my rescue?"

He stood looking at her for a minute, as if pondering the question "I have to admit I did think twice about it. I would have much rather remained on my deck drinking my ice cold beer. But I couldn't very well just leave you out there to drown, now could I?"

"Oh, I'm sorry for disrupting your beer drinking! she spat "but you needn't have bothered. I was managing quite well on my own."

A teasing smile played on his lips, "I could see that," his eyes dropped to her dress. He liked how it clung invitingly to her body, doing very little to hide what lay beneath. He took a deep breath as his eyes caught sight of her taut nipples pressing invitingly against the wet fabric. He deliberately let his eyes wander her body. Her face flushed, as he boldly took in the soft curve of her hips and her near naked breasts. He returned his eyes to her face. Wrapping her arms across her chest. quivering at his obvious appraisal of her, she met his eyes in a challenging stare.

His lips turned up at the corners ever so slightly. "You know a simple' thank you' would have sufficed," he said, enjoying her obvious discomfort.

She gave him a forced smile, "thank... you."

He grinned, "Now that wasn't so hard, was it?"

A cold shiver ran up the length of her body. His brow creased as he took in her pale colour and the heightened colour of her lips. "You should come up to the house and get out of those wet clothes."

She glanced over his shoulder at the house nestled back against a line of trees and gave a cynical little laugh,

"What makes you think I would go anywhere with you?"
He stood silently assessing her. "I don't really care one way or the other." He said, casually shrugging his shoulders. "The choice is yours."
He grinned, "But if I were you, I'd think very hard before turning down my offer."
Her eyes narrowed as her body gave another little shiver, "Oh you would, would you? And why would that be?"
He let his eyes travel her body. "Your dress, it doesn't leave much to the imagination." He said staring boldly at her. A quick vision of her naked flashed to the forefront of his mind.
A pink tinge crept onto her cheeks as she drew her arms tighter around her body.
"I don't trust you."
He gave her a deliciously gorgeous smile, causing her heart to flutter. "That's a little ironic, don't you think, since I just saved your life?"
Her mouth opened then closed again.
His eyes locked on hers. "You don't have to worry. You're not my type."
She swiped the back of her hand across her forehead, "Whew! What a relief. Well, you'll be pleased to know that you're not exactly mine either."
He grinned, "My offer still stands. Take it or leave it." he replied before turning and making his way up the beach.
She stood for a few minutes watching his retreating back. Giving an exasperated huff she reluctantly followed him. A fine specimen he may be, but his personality certainly had some very big flaws. As much as she hated to agree,

he was right about one thing. It would be sheer torture to walk home in her wet clingy dress, and probably a little indecent. What choice did she have?

# Chapter two

By the time she got to the path he was nowhere to be seen. Why was she even considering going to the house of a complete stranger and a rude one at that? So he had saved her life, as he so begrudgingly pointed out. With some reluctance, she made her way up the bush lined path. When she reached the end she drew to a stop. The house looked a lot bigger up close. It was two storied, with two upper balconies. Its rich timber exterior seemed to blend effortlessly into its surroundings. The house faced out towards the bay. Huge floor to ceiling windows ran along the entire front of the house, giving it vast, uninterrupted views of the bay and surrounding coastline. The wooden decks seemed to stretch out endlessly towards the sea. A row of dense trees lined the back of the property, forming a thick wall of seclusion. Glancing up at the balcony above she realised he must have been up there when he saw her fall. What if he hadn't been watching? Her body gave a little shudder, she didn't even want to think about it. The distant sound of the waves breaking against the shoreline could be heard in the distance. Everything thing about the house screamed money. Curiosity drew her toward the front porch. Her hand glided over the twisted length of driftwood, which had been used a handrail for the steps. Glancing toward the coast, she wondered if they had come from the bay. Suddenly she felt like an intruder. The little voice in the back of her head began to scream at her to leave. Turning around she hurried back down the path.

"So you're not coming in, then?"

She stopped, glancing up she found him looking down at her from the balcony above. Her face heated "I don't want to put you to any trouble."

"It's a bit late for that? Don't you think?"

"I guess so..., all the more reason why I should leave." He shrugged his shoulders in that annoying non committal way," Suit yourself. Stay or go, I don't really care which" he replied, turning and disappearing from view. A cold shiver ran up the length of her body. The sun had barely begun to set and already the temperature had dropped quite dramatically. It was a good hour's walk home and in a wet dress and no shoes, probably longer. Reluctantly she turned back to the house. As she climbed the stairs, she half expected a beautiful blonde haired wife to materialise with two perfect little children in tow. She hesitated at the door; leaning forward, she peered inside.

A gasp escaped her lips when she caught sight of her reflection in a mirror hanging on the wall. "Damn it" she cursed, as she attempted to draw her fingers through her tangled mass of hair in a futile attempt to fix her dishevelled appearance. With an deep sigh, she gave up. Gathering up her wet, sand laden dress so as not to mark the beautifully polished wooden floors she stepped across the threshold. The timber was warm beneath her feet.

"Hello" she called, as she slowly made her way up the passage. When she reached the end, it opened up into a large sun filled room. A set of wooden French doors stood between her and a large covered veranda.

"Hello," her call was again met with silence.

The late afternoon sun streamed in through the windows warming the room. The doors to the veranda stood wide open. She stepped outside. A quick glance around confirmed that she was alone. Moving down the short flight of stairs she found herself standing on a quaint little paved path. She stole a quick glance back at the house. Giving little thought to his privacy, she followed it. The soft sound of trickling water caught her attention, drawing her deeper into the garden. A small stream appeared beside her. Now intrigued, she followed it and was pleasantly surprised when it opened out onto a large oval shaped pond. She stood mesmerised as the sunlight danced across the surface of the water. Rocks and vegetation encased the pond, creating a secluded little glen. Her eyes were drawn to the large bronze statue of a naked woman which took pride of place in the centre pond. The woman stood poised on her tiptoes, her arms stretched up towards the darkening sky. She held a lily in her hands from which water spilled, trickling down over her form. It added a soft sensuality to an already very romantic setting. It certainly wasn't what she would have expected from a man like him. She smiled, the naked lady maybe, but the rest, no.

Startling at a noise behind her she turned to find him standing on the path watching her. She gave him an apologetic smile, "I'm sorry... I really didn't mean to pry." His stomach tightened as he was momentarily taken in by her wide eyed innocence.

"I did invite you in."

"That doesn't give me the right to snoop."

Her rich auburn hair hung in tangled curls about her pale shoulders. There was something about her, a soft vulnerability that appealed to him, yet he had also seen the fire in her eyes. He found her rather intriguing. Her eyes shone excitedly, "No one would ever know that this little piece of paradise even existed."

His eyes narrowed, "And that's the way I would like to keep it, if it's all the same to you."

Noting his surly tone she glanced up at him, her beautiful green eyes instantly drawing him in. She gave a little nervous laugh, "Your secret's safe with me," she replied, stepping over to the edge of the pond and crouching down to trail her fingers lightly through the cool still water. All the past aggravation slipped from her mind. "I would love to have a garden like this, but there isn't the room at home. I have to be content with planters and pots." He gave an acknowledging grunt. As she slowly rose to her feet, she felt his eyes still upon her. The setting sun silhouetted her body against the thin fabric of her dress. He drew in a long deep breath. Her nipples hardened under his bold stare. It had been a long time since she had felt the thrill of desire. Two years ago she had made a promise to herself, vowing to never again let herself feel what she was feeling right now.

He gave an impatient huff and turned away, determined not to let himself fall for her obvious charms. He was sick and tired of being introduced to woman that he didn't even particularly like, and who seemed to be more interested in his money than anything else. Hadn't he already proved himself? Wasn't the fact that he had managed to save the family business from total ruin enough for her? Why was it that his mother found it necessary to interfere in his personal life as well? The way she was pushing him, you would think he was past his prime. At twenty nine he was far from it. He glanced back at her. He wondered if his mother had had anything to do with this woman landing on his doorstep. Getting someone to nearly drown themselves, he hoped was way beyond even his mother's capabilities. He smiled taking in her bedraggled appearance. No, this certainly wasn't his mother's style at all. There was no way she would approve of this woman. Adriana glanced up and caught him smiling. His eyes softened. A few strands of his dark blonde hair had drifted down across his forehead. Her heart gave a sudden flutter. She liked being admired, especially by a man like him.

"This garden couldn't be more perfect. Does your wife do the gardening?"

His stomach knotted, the word gold-digger sprang to mind? He brushed the thought aside. Looking at her she didn't seem the desperate type; a little emotional maybe. His eyes narrowed watching for her reaction "I do the gardens myself."

Her cheeks flushed "oh, I'm sorry..., I just assumed."

"Well, you assumed wrong..., single life is a lot less complicated," he snapped, as he turned to leave. "Will you be wanting to take a shower?" he asked not bothering to look back.

"Oh, um... yes please. That would  be great., thank you." He replied with a grunt as he disappeared down the path. Why was it that he could be so nice one minute and so damn arrogant the next? What was his problem? No wonder he was still single. Maybe he was one of those men who had a string of females at his beck and call. If his looks were anything to go by, that would certainly be plausible. She gave a quick shake of her head. What he did, or with whom he did it, certainly wasn't any of her business. As she made her way back along the path she found herself wondering what it would be like to be with a man like him. Would he even be able to commit himself to one female? She gave a little snort, thinking it would be very unlikely. Stepping up onto the veranda she poked her head in the door. The room was empty. He didn't really want her here, that was plainly obvious. Her bare feet padded across the wooden floor. As she waited for his return she felt the urge to have a little look around. The interior of the room was stark, more like something you would expect to find in a modern city apartment. It was very sparsely furnished with a clever use of leather, chrome and glass. All very sterile, she thought as she walked around the room. It was beyond tidy, nothing out of place, except for the fine grains of sand that had dropped from her feet. At the very least she had expected to see a discarded magazine or a used coffee mug. She bent down and ran her hand over the coffee table in front of her; her hand came away clean. He was either a neat freak or he had a cleaner. Her eyes were drawn to the small sculpture that stood in the centre of the coffee table. A naked man and  woman intertwined in an erotic embrace. Now that definitely seemed more like him. The painting hanging on the wall above the leather sofa caught her attention. Her brow creased as she stood studying it. Suddenly it registered. She had sold it two months previously. Surely she would have remembered a man like him coming into the store? Or would she? The way she had been feeling lately Brad Pitt could have walked into the store and she probably wouldn't have noticed. With a shrug of her shoulders she turned to scrutinize the rest of the room. Her eyes moved to the large glass topped dining table. Eight padded leather chairs were tucked neatly around it. A huge vase of freshly cut flowers stood in the middle of the table. Unable to curb her curiosity, she walked toward the kitchen and was shocked to see that it was bigger than her mother's kitchen, sitting room and dining room combined. What would a single man need with such monstrous kitchen? It was hard not to feel envious as she took in the impressive stainless steel gas cooker, the huge double door fridge and state of the art dishwasher. The coffee maker was top of the line, too along with the microwave oven. A huge island bench with a breakfast bar attached dominated the room. Her fingertips glided over the cool black granite surface. Six chrome stools with padded black leather cushions were neatly tucked under one side of the bench. Obviously no expense had been spared in this kitchen. Much like the other room, it had floor to ceiling windows along one wall giving an expansive view of the coastline. She could almost imagine herself standing at the sink preparing a meal as she gazed out at the bay. A cynical little laugh escaped her lips, "In your dreams" she whispered to herself.

A door closed somewhere down the hallway; she hurried back to the other room and stepped outside quickly, moving to the far end of the veranda. A cold shiver ran through her body as the cool breeze blew her damp dress against her skin. Her gaze drifted to the bay, would she ever be free of the guilt which clung so fiercely to her? It was her fault that her daughter was growing up without a father. Her eyes moistened, "I will always be yours" she whispered softly into the wind.

"Who will always be yours?"

Blinking back her tears, she turned to face him, "Oh..., nothing..," her face flushed. He was leaning against the doorframe wearing only a towel which was slung low around his hips. A light trail of hair started just below his navel and disappeared below his towel. The late afternoon sun glistened off his beautifully bronzed damp skin. Her heart rate accelerated as an involuntary little quiver ran up the length of her body. Her eyes were drawn to his torso. Broad shoulders and strong defined lines accentuated the muscle on his lean, smooth athletic frame.

The corner of his lips twitched ever so slightly. "I brought you some dry clothes and a towel. The shower is all yours if you want it? He said holding out a bundle of clothes with two towels neatly folded on top. "It's down the hall, first door on your right."

Ensuring to keep her eyes averted, and making a conscious effort not to touch him she took the bundle from his hands. The faint smell of soap and freshly cut pine drifted off him as she brushed past.

Unnerved by her reaction to him, she hurried into the bathroom locking the door behind her. Resting her back against the door she waited for her heart rate to settle. Giving an annoyed huff she pushed away from the door. What was going on with her? Only minutes ago she had promised her husband her lifelong devotion, the next she was having unwanted thoughts about a man she had only just met. Unbuttoning her dress, she let it fall to the floor, then she slipped off her underwear. Catching her refection in the mirror she gave a long sigh. The beautiful young woman she had once been had all but disappeared. In her place was an empty shell. The only time she felt joy was when she was with her daughter. Her heart had been crushed and it felt as if it would never heal. Over the past two years she had made little effort with her appearance. It was her way of punishing herself for the part she had played in her husband and son's deaths. Her shoulders slumped. She was only twenty eight, but felt years older. Grief had begun to take its toll and she had no idea if she would ever be able to recover. Noticing a discarded tee shirt draped over the side of the bath she reached down and picked it up and held it against her face, breathing in the masculine scent. Tears filled her eyes; she missed having a man in her life. The thought of being alone forever now seemed daunting. She threw the shirt down. It was her mistake and she would have to live with it. Turning on the shower she stepped in. Her body gave a little shiver as the warm water trickled down over her cool damp skin.

When she finally felt composed enough to leave the safety of the bathroom, she headed back out to the veranda. He was leaning against the railing, looking intently out at the ocean. To her relief, he was wearing a pair of jeans and a tee-shirt. Stepping out of the door she made her way to the railing ensuring to keep her eyes focused on the bay. At the sound of her approach he turned to look at her.

"How are the clothes?"

She gave him a tentative smile, as she forced herself to look at him. "A little on the big side..., but appreciated all the same."

His facial expression gave little indication to his mood as his eyes boldly studied her. How was it that she could look so damned sexy wearing a pair of his sweatpants and a simple flannel shirt? "Glad to hear it," he said, noting that she had rolled up the pant legs. His eyes were momentarily drawn to her slender calves and ankles.

"I borrowed this tie off the robe behind the door. I hope you don't mind. I needed something to help keep them up."

His eyes travelled the length of her body. He thought the flannel shirt looked a damn sight better on her than it did on him, the coarse flannel a stark contrast against the smooth paleness of her skin. "I like the shirt."

She gave a nervous little laugh, "I'm thinking of starting a new trend." The shirt was too long, so she had knotted the ends at her waist and rolled up the sleeves. He tugged at the knot, "I think you might just have a winner there." he said lightly brushing his finger tips up her arm. Her body gave an involuntary little quiver. Feeling a little out of her depth, she stepped away from him and turned to look out at the bay. Tension was beginning to build up in her shoulders. It had definitely been a mistake to come here.

"Would you like a hot drink?"

"Yes please," she replied a little too quickly.

"Hot chocolate, tea or coffee, the choice is yours."

"Hot chocolate, would be great thanks."

His eyes roamed her delicate frame. Was she even aware of how desirable she looked right now? He moved closer, finding it hard to draw his eyes away. A sudden jolt of wanting shot through him as she turned and looked up at him, her eyes holding his momentarily, hinting at something deeper. Her lips parted ever so slightly and he suddenly found himself wondering what it would be like to kiss her. Her eyes shone like emerald green pools and he found himself slowly being drawn into their depths. Her eyes widened and she quickly dropped them, snapping him out of his trance. Giving a little annoyed grunt he brushed past her. What was it about her that had him all twisted up in knots? "I had better get you that drink."

She nodded sucking in her breath as his arm brushed against hers. "What are you doing?" she muttered to herself. In the short time she had been in his company he had managed to trigger feelings that she was sure she had locked away forever.


He re-appeared moments later holding a mug, "one hot chocolate as ordered."

Reaching out, she took the mug from him. Her hand brushed against his and she nearly dropped it as a hot tingle shot across her skin. Her fingers tightened around the mug. She dared a quick glance up at him, "Thanks" Their eyes locked, a shot of desire flared up inside her. His eyes darkened, as he reached out to brush away a stray lock of hair that had fallen across her cheek.

Her eyes widened, "Don't..., please."

He gave an exasperated sigh, and reached out and tucked the hair behind her ear. Placing her hand on the rail she tried to steady her shattered nerves.

His eyes were drawn to the wedding band on her finger. The fact that she was married should have made him back off, but for reasons unbeknown to him it didn't. There was an unseen force drawing him toward her and he wasn't sure he liked it. He stepped away from her and moved to the rail, not willing to admit to what his body was so obviously telling him.

"What is it with you anyway?"

She glanced up at him. His cold calculating eyes were once again focused on her.

"I'm not sure what you mean."

He gave one of his impatient huffs. "Why do you spend so much of your time staring out at the ocean?"

"I don't."

He rolled his eyes "Oh come on. I've seen you out there," he waved his hand towards the shore, "at least twice a week for the last four months."

She took a sip of her drink, shifting nervously. "I don't think that's any of your business."

He gave a sarcastic little laugh, "You nearly drowned yourself today. If it wasn't for me, you'd probably be floating out there as fish fodder."

His words hit a raw nerve, she choked back a sob. "Look, I am thankful that you rescued me, but my personal life is none of your business."

He leant over and lightly ran his fingers down the side of her cheek "I might be able to help."

She recoiled from his touch, slamming her mug down on the railing and spilling some of the contents. "I asked you not to do that."

He grinned "I know."

Her eyes narrowed, "Look I don't know what your game is but I don't need nor want your help."

His face hardened, "I just thought maybe..."

"What? That I'd be so grateful I would sleep with you. Is that it?"

"No! Of course not," he grinned, "but I certainly wouldn't be opposed to the idea."

Her hands shifted to her hips, "You know, you might be used to having women falling all over you, but I can assure you, this one certainly won't be."

He stepped closer. "You're quite sure about that?" he whispered softly in her ear.

Her body tensed. "You're nothing but an arrogant pig. I could have drowned today, and all you're thinking about is if you can get me into bed or not."

He grinned, she was so easy to rile, "You can't blame a man for trying, and anyway who said anything about a bed?"

"That's..., the kind of response I would expect from a man like you."

"A man like me?"

"Attractive, self assured, arrogant, non committal, rude, and thinks he can have any woman he desires. Need I go on?"

"So you think I'm attractive."

Her hands went to her hips, "No!"

He raised his eyebrows.

She gave an exasperated sigh. "Looks aren't everything." she snapped.

His eyes drifted to her ring. What the hell was he doing? "Look, I'm sorry."

Her eyes narrowed, "I'm sure you are." It had been a very emotional day for her, and she was struggling to keep her emotions in check. The last thing she wanted was to turn into a blithering mess, in front of him. "I think it might be best if I leave." she turned towards the door.

His hand closed around her arm, "wait..., please, I'll drive you home."

She shook his arm off. "I don't think so. I'd rather walk than have to endure another minute in your company. I'll return your clothes in a day or two," she replied fighting to contain her tears as she hurried to the front door.

He shook his head. Why were women always so damn sensitive? He clenched his fists, knowing he shouldn't have pushed her. Cursing he rushed out the door after her. She was making a fast exit down the path. "There is no rush on the clothes, just whenever you happen to be out here next."

She gritted her teeth; was he still making fun of her? she stopped and turned back to face him "You know just because you rescued me today doesn't give you the right to be a bastard."

He held his hand to his chest, "That's the thanks I get for saving your life.? Next time I might just leave you to drown."

She glared up at him "there won't be a next time."

He gave her an annoying smirk. Tears spilt over her cheeks as she quickly turned away and stomped off down the path. Why couldn't he just mind his own damned business? "He's certainly a lot less appealing than he looks," she mumbled to herself, as she made her way down to the beach.

He cursed under his breath as he watched her disappear down the path. He shouldn't have chased her off. She was right. Over the last couple of years he had become a little arrogant and at times downright rude. He certainly hadn't been bought up to treat women that way. Unknowingly, it had become his defence against the countless women his mother flung his way. He watched the retreating figure racing across the sand. He shrugged, maybe it was for the best, he certainly wasn't in the habit of pursing  married women and wasn't about to start.

# Chapter Three

Four days had passed since she had stormed out of his house and he couldn't stop thinking about her. He juggled the gold locket in his hand. He had been so sure she would come back for it. Snapping it open he looked at the images again. A handsome looking dark haired man and a young boy looked back at him. Was it her husband and son? He clicked it closed. The way he had treated her gnawed at him. He had hoped she would come back so he could at the very least apologise for his behaviour. As the days passed, he realised he was waiting in vain. He glanced down at the locket. It was all he had to go on. He hadn't even had the decency to ask her name. His clothes had appeared two days later folded neatly and left in a pile outside his door.

Adriana sat in front of the mirror; she placed her hand where her locket used to sit. By now it was probably lying buried in the sand somewhere. She hadn't dared go back and look for it, for fear she might run into him again. He had stirred emotions in her that she thought she had securely locked away. Suddenly the door burst open. A little green eyed girl ran into the room, her soft ringlets bouncing around her shoulders.

"Mommy, mommy, look what g...andma gave me," she held up her hand to show Adriana the little silver bracelet encircling her tiny wrist.

"It has my name on it."

Adriana smiled "So it does," she picked her daughter up and hugged her tightly. "It's beautiful darling, you're a very lucky girl. I hope you said thank you to Grandma." She wiggled in her mother's arms, "mommy, I'm getting squashed."

Adriana loosened her grip, "sorry baby, I just love you so much."

The little girl reached up and kissed her cheek, "I lub you too."

Tears sprung to Adriana eyes. "Don't cry mommy, it's my birfday."

Adriana wiped away her tears, "it's only because I love you so much."

Her daughter wiggled free and slipped off her knee. "G...andma said for you to hurry or you'll miss my party."

Adriana smiled as she watched her daughter scamper excitedly down the hall. "Hey, Madi." the little girl stopped, turning back to look at her mother. Adriana blew her a kiss. Madi giggled as she pretended to grab it and hold it against her chest, then quickly turned and continued up the hall. Adriana wondered how she would have coped without her. Looking back into the mirror she began to apply her makeup. Today she would make a special effort, just for Madison.

Satisfied with her reflection, she headed for the kitchen. "Is everything okay in here?" she asked as she entered.

Her mother turned looking a little flustered, but couldn't help smiling when she saw her daughter.

"You look beautiful."

Adriana smiled "thanks Mom, so do you need any help?"

"No. I think I have everything under control. There is one thing you could do though, nip up to the store and get a bottle of cream. It's the one thing I forgot."

"Sure thing, are you positive there is nothing else you need?"

"No I think that's it."

Adriana turned to leave, "I'll be back shortly."

Her mother turned back to what she was doing. "Please don't be too long. I don't want the guests to start arriving and you're not here."

Adriana laid a reassuring hand on her mother's shoulder. "You worry far too much. We still have a good three quarters of an hour before the guests start arriving."

Her mother glanced around at her, "Sorry..., it's been a long time since I've hosted a children's party." It was nice to see that Adriana had paid a little bit more attention to her appearance. It had been quite some time since she had seen her wearing any makeup at all.

Adriana headed for the door, "See you soon."

Adriana strolled down the road, enjoying the feel of the sun on her face. Madison was turning three today. How quickly time had passed. It seemed like only yesterday that she was holding her newborn baby in her arms. A lump caught in her throat as visions of her husband's beaming face entered her thoughts. He had loved his daughter so much, why did life have to be so cruel? Madison was now growing up without a father, all because of her mother's stupidity. Picking up her pace she pushed away her negative thoughts; if she started crying now it would ruin her makeup. Her daughter deserved a wonderful birthday and she was going to make damn sure she got it.

Hayden drove down the street for the fourth time, not knowing where to go next. He had asked around town but no one seemed to be able to help him out. Without a name, it was like trying to find a needle in a haystack. He slammed on his brakes. An impatient car horn sounded behind him. He glanced across at a woman exiting the store. She turned at the sound of the horn. He couldn't believe his luck. His eyes followed her as she continued on down the path. He almost hadn't recognized her. He checked ahead of him for a parking space. There weren't any. She turned down a side street. He cursed, indicating at the last minute and swerving into the other lane; another car horn sounded. Waving an apology out the window he waited for the traffic to clear, hoping she wouldn't disappear. His tyres squealed as he shot through a narrow gap in the traffic and entered the street. His body relaxed a little when he spied her climbing the front steps to a house a little further up the street. He drove slowly down the road, pulling up opposite the house. It was a very basic two storey semi dethatched unit, that looked very much like the rest of the houses in the street. The gardens however, looked amazing and the front steps were adorned with pots overflowing with brightly coloured flowers. He put his hand on the door handle, and found himself hesitating. Slipping his hand inside his shirt pocket, he drew out the locket he had carefully wrapped in tissue paper. She would want it back, he was sure of it. If he had only been a little more civil to her, then maybe he wouldn't feel so awkward about knocking on her front door.

He crossed the street and made his way up the front steps. He stood for a minute looking at the closed door then lifted his hand and rapped loudly. After a few minutes the door opened. He had run through what he was going to say so many times, but he needn't have bothered. The door opened. A little girl stood staring at him. Her green eyes blinked at him innocently. She was fair skinned and had long, dark hair which cascaded around her shoulders. A small sprinkling of freckles trailed across her little button nose. Her small pink lips pouted slightly. There was certainly no doubting whose child she was.

Her little face lit up into a smile.

"Hello..., are you here for my party?" She asked looking at him curiously.

"Oh! No sorry, I'm not... I was wondering if I could speak with your Mommy," he hesitated "or Daddy."

She put her little hands on her hips. He smiled, having seen that stance before.

"Mommy's making my cake and my Daddy's in hea...vin with da an..., an...gilles."

His brow creased, as he tried to decipher what she had just said, "oh the angels."

She nodded, "It's my Birfday."

He crouched down in front of her "Is it now, well Happy Birthday. How old are you?"

Her little pink lips turned up into a delightful smile, "I'm a big girl now. I'm free."

Unable to contain his amusement he laughed. "My goodness, you are a big girl. Are you having a party?"

She jumped up and down excitedly "yep."


Adriana could hear her daughter talking to someone at the front door. She rinsed and dried her hands and headed up the hall.

"Madi, who are you talk...." she stopped mid sentence.

"Mommy, this man wants to talk to you."

Adriana stared wide eyed as he slowly drew to his feet.

"What, oh..., um..., thank you Madi, but you know you shouldn't talk to strangers without checking with mommy first. Now how about you go and see how grandma's doing..? I'll only be a minute."

Madison's lip drooped, "but he said happy birthday."

Adriana smiled, as she ran her hand over Madison's hair "It's okay baby. Thank you."

"Ok, bye" Madison called, as she skipped up the hall. He smiled as he watched her leave, now unsure what to say, "Cute kid."

Adriana eyed him suspiciously, "What was it you wanted?" She asked glancing up the hallway. The last thing she needed was a game of twenty questions with her mother, "And how did you find me?"

He smiled "I've been looking for you."

Her heart skipped a beat. "It was only by sheer luck that I spotted you coming out of the store." Words escaped her. "I bought your dress back." His eyes locked with hers. Her breath escaped her lungs. "You had better come in then" she said rather more abruptly than she had intended, as she stepped back from the door, taking a deep breath. The last thing she wanted was him knowing how much his presence was affecting her. He stepped over the threshold, not seeming to notice her abruptness, or choosing to ignore it, she wasn't sure which. A soft scent of apricots filled his senses as he passed by her. They entered the sitting room; it was small, but it had a homely feel about it, something he had always felt lacking in his family home. They stood facing one another, neither of them knowing quite what to say. Her palms moistened. He ran a quick apprising eye over her. She looked so enticing in her soft flowing deep green sleeveless dress, which he had to admit matched her eyes perfectly. The hem of the dress stopped mid thigh giving him a good view of her long slender legs. The fitted bodice hugged against her body and was cut low enough in the front to accentuate the line of her neck and give him a small glimpse of cleavage. A delicate silver butterfly pendant hung from a fine silver chain resting lightly against her collarbone.

"You look... amazing" he said unable to take his eyes off her.

Her brows drew together. It was hard enough controlling herself, without him throwing her unnecessary compliments.

"You have my dress?"

"Oh right..., here. "he said handing it to her. "I had it washed and pressed."

She glanced up at him, "You didn't have to."

"I know, but I owe you at least that."

Her face heated. "I also thought you might want this." he held out the small tissue wrapped package.

Her body stiffened, "I can't take that."

"It's not a gift. I think it belongs to you."

She slipped it from his hand, ensuring not to touch him. Carefully she unfolded the tissue and when she saw what it contained she dropped down onto the chair. "Where did you find it?" she asked, tears already beginning to well in her eyes.

He wasn't quite sure what to do. He sat down beside her and placed a hand on her arm, but quickly removed it when he felt her stiffen. Getting back to his feet he moved away, feeling at a loss as to what to do as tears began to flood down her cheeks.

"Um... it was caught in your dress."

At that moment Madison entered the room, stopping abruptly when she saw her mother's tears. She glared up at him. "Did you make Mommy cry?"

Before he could answer she ran from the room calling to her grandmother. "G...andma, gandma. The man made Mommy cry."

By the time they had both returned to the room, he had left. Patricia sat down on the couch beside her daughter and put her arm around her shoulder.

"What's the matter, love?"

Adriana held out the locket for her to see, "I thought I had lost it."

Her mother placed her hand over Adrianna's and held it there, wishing more than anything that her daughter would let go of the guilt. Madison climbed up onto her mother's knee.

"Was he a bad man, Mommy?"

Adriana gave her a reassuring smile, "No darling, he wasn't a bad man. He just returned something that mommy thought she had lost, that's all."

"Can I still have my party?"

Adrianna wiped her eyes, "Yes darling, of course we can. Mommy just needs to go upstairs for a minute. When I come down, I'll finish your cake."

Madison gave her mother a kiss then slid off her knee. Patricia stood up and took her hand.

"Come on Madi, let's go and finish mixing the icing, so it's all ready for when Mommy comes back down."

Adriana looked up at her mother, "Thanks Mom."

"Just hurry back, the guests will start arriving soon."

Adriana climbed the stairs and entered her room. Undoing the clasp of the necklace, she placed it back in her jewellery box, then fastened the locket around her neck. Maybe one day she would be able to take it off, but for now it was where it was supposed to be. Her fingers closed around it. It still hurt to think about them. Getting up, she walked over to the window and was surprised to see him still sitting in his car on the opposite side of the road. How ungrateful she had been; he had gone to the trouble of finding her. He pulled away from the curb, she watched until he turned out of the street.

Well, that had certainly been a little awkward, and hadn't gone quite how he had planned. At least now he knew where she lived and that she was a widow. His brow creased,. With a child. He thumped the steering wheel, realising he still hadn't asked her name.

# Chapter Four

As Adriana unlocked the door to her store, a smile touched her lips. This had always been her dream. With the life insurance money, she had been able to secure a future for Madison and herself. As she glanced around the store, a sense of pride washed over her. All her hard work had finally begun to pay off. Flicking on the light switch, the store was instantly transformed into a brightly lit Aladdin's cave full of delightful works of art, all handcrafted by local artists. Slipping off her shoes she made her way to the centre of the room and stood looking around her. This was where she felt most at peace. A glass bowl on a shelf in front of her caught her eye. She walked over and moved it a few inches to the right. For the next half an hour she dusted, vacuumed and reset displays.

Finally it was time to open. At exactly nine o'clock she unlocked the doors. Stepping outside she took a minute to absorb her surroundings. Rockland's main street was lined with quaint old fashioned buildings and unique little stores. She loved it here; everyone was so friendly and the whole town had a very homely feel about it. It was one of the reasons her mother had never felt the need to leave. She glanced up at the brilliant blue sky. There wasn't a cloud to be seen. The sun's rays were already beginning to warm the pavement beneath her feet, summer was finally here.

"Good morning Adriana," a man called from across the street.

She smiled and gave a wave. "Hi Ross. I think it's going to be nice day."

He tossed a hand towel over his shoulder, giving her a warm smile, "Sure is. If you feel in need of an ice cream later, pop over."

"I might just take you up on that. I think you're in luck, looks like we might be in for a bit of a heat wave, great for the ice cream trade."

"Here's hoping. So I'll see you later then," he said waving as he turned back to his store.

Adriana stepped back inside. Ross had been so supportive when her husband and son had gone missing. Even before she had thought about opening a store, many an hour had been spent with him simply talking. Now that she was just across the street it had become their little ritual. Every Monday and Thursday she would head over for an ice cream and a chat. However, just lately she had been getting the feeling that he wanted more out of the relationship than she did.


When lunch time finally arrived, she locked up the store and headed across to the ice-cream parlour. The bell jingled as she entered.

"Don't panic, just me" she called as Ross appeared through the doorway. His face instantly lit up when he saw her. He wasn't what you would call strikingly handsome, but with his olive skin, dark wavy hair, soft brown eyes and, to die for, smile, he had his share of admirers.

"You came?"

"Of course I did. You promised ice cream."

He grinned "I thought food was the way to a man's heart."

"I don't consider ice cream a food, and its dessert," she replied laughing.

"So what'll it be today?"

"I think I'll go for chocolate ripple today."

Picking up a cone he moved over to the freezer. The young girl behind the counter rolled her eyes.

"You know I could do that."

He smiled, "I know, but it's sort of a tradition." He walked around the counter and handed Adriana her ice cream.

"Let's go and sit out the back in the shade."

He was so easy to be around, she thought as she followed him through the back of the store. He held the door open for her. She walked out and sat on the seat in the shade. The ice cream was already starting to melt. With a casualness only he could manage, he dropped down beside her and leant in to take a lick of her ice cream. She snatched it away. "You know you own the store right? You could get your own."

"Just thought you needed a hand." He patted his flat stomach "and watching the waist line at the same time." Her tongue licked right around the base quickly eliminating all drips, "See, all under control, now keep your tongue to yourself."

He grinned, "You just let me know if you need any more help."

"I think I can take it from here..., but, thanks for the offer."

Leaning back in the chair he looked across at her. "So..., how have things been at home? How's my little Madi and Patricia?

"Everything's fine; Madi turned three the other day. I can't believe how quickly time has passed. And Mom, well she's great as always." She paused, deciding on a change of subject "I made a couple of big sales this morning. Which is always good."

He sensed what she was trying to do. "You miss him, don't you?"

Her eyes glistened, "That's a silly question. Of course I do. I always will," she snapped.

They sat quietly for a minute.

"I'm sorry Ross, it's just that some days are harder than others."

His hand moved to her knee, "you don't have to explain. I understand. But you should know it's okay to move on.

Miss them by all means, but don't put your life on hold. Alistair wouldn't have wanted that."

"I wish it was that easy."

"It could be easy Adriana, if you let it. All you have to do is take that first step,"

"Oh and you think it's that simple?"

He studied her, "Adriana."

She glanced up, not liking the look on his face. Her stomach tightened. Hadn't she warned herself this was coming?

"It's been two years now since,  well you know, and I was just wondering is there any chance of us being..., more than just friend?."

He saw her tense, "I...  I don't mean right now, but maybe sometime down the track, could you see us together?"

Her stomach churned. How to let him down without hurting what they already had. A big drip of ice cream fell on her skirt and she didn't even notice.

"Look Ross, you're a nice guy..., but honestly I'm just not ready. I'm not sure if I ever will be. Can't we just leave things as they are...," she felt the need to soften the blow, "for now at least?" Another drip fell on her skirt.

Ross smiled as he leaned across and took a big lick of her ice cream.

"Hey, that's not fair, you distracted me."

He grinned, "You were the one letting it drip. Look I'm sorry for bringing it up. Can we just pretend I didn't say anything and we'll leave it at that? Just promise me one thing,  if ever you feel ready to move on, please let me be the first to know."

"I promise you'll be the first to know," she said placing a little kiss on his cheek.

They spent the next half an hour laughing and joking together, and when the time came to go back she was reluctant to leave.

"Ross" He turned to her, "I love spending time with you, you know that, don't you? You were there for me when I needed it the most. That means a lot. I'm sorry I can't give you what you want, but it's too soon."

He patted her knee, "Don't worry yourself about it. I can wait for as long as it takes."

Her brow creased, "I don't want you to wait. Don't you see? What if you missed out on the ideal woman, all because you were waiting for one that may never be ready? So please, I'm asking you don't wait for me I couldn't bear it."

He let out a long sigh, "Fine. If the ideal woman comes along I'll snap her up right away. Happy now?"

She threw her arms around him and gave him a hug, "Yes, this won't change things between us will it?"

He rubbed his chin as if considering it.

"Hmmm..., maybe... I might need to start charging you for the ice creams. You know, so nobody gets the wrong idea."

She punched his arm, "Ha, ha very funny. So same time Thursday alright for you?" she said, getting to her feet.

He smiled reassuringly.

"See you Thursday and don't forget to bring your purse."

Hopefully he hadn't been too hurt by her rejection. She loved him deeply, but not in that way.

The rest of the day was fairly uneventful, until she was about to shut up store. As she made her way to the door, an older lady and a young boy entered. Adriana glanced up at the clock. Why was it customers always felt the need to shop at closing time? The lady walked over and began to examine one of the items on display. Adriana turned the sign on the door to read 'closed', then went back and settled herself on the chair behind the counter. She started to get a little agitated as the hands began to creep around the clock. Her mother had made arrangements to go out, so she couldn't be late. The woman took her time looking over the pieces. Adriana wondered if she was doing it deliberately. The phone rang, startling her. She reached across the counter and picked it up, already knowing who it would be.

"Hello, Madison's Handcrafts."

"Adriana where are you? My ride will be here any minute."

"I'm sorry Mom. I'll be home as soon as I can. I just have one last customer."

"Just tell them you're closed, and to come back tomorrow."

"Okay Mom, look don't worry I'll see you soon."

Adriana placed the phone down and looked up at the clock. It was already quarter to six, way past closing time. Adriana got off her stool and walked over to the woman.

"Excuse me, but I'm actually closed. I open again at nine tomorrow, if you would like to come back then." The woman turned and fixed her with a cold grey stare that bored right through her.

"The door was unlocked was it not? The 'Open' sign was out, therefore if I'm not mistaken, that means you are open. Is that not correct?"

Adriana faltered a little, "Well yes, but I was about to close when you walked in."

"Well, surely you can do that when I'm finished," the woman hissed, as she deliberately turned to study the bowl in front of her in great detail.

The hairs on the back of Adriana's neck prickled. "Look, I'm sorry, but I'm going to have to ask you to leave."

The woman turned on her, "You obviously have no idea who I am. Do you?"

Adriana looked a little stunned "Should I? Not that that would make any difference; I would still be asking you to leave," replied Adriana her anger flaring.

"Come on Grandma, let's just go" urged the young boy beside her.

The woman frowned at him. "You never back down. That's not the Radcliff way. You need to start thinking like a Radcliff boy. Your name means something in this town."

Adriana let out a small sigh. She had heard enough. Who did this woman think she was? If she thought she could come into her store and throw her weight around, she had another thing coming. Adriana moved to the door and opened it.

"I'm sorry to hear that, because I would like you to leave, now!"

The woman's face contorted with anger. "How dare you

order me out of your store like some common low life. You are making a big mistake, girly. I know a lot of people in this town and can make life very difficult for you."

Adriana placed her hands on her hips.

"Are you threatening me? Because I don't take kindly to being threatened,"

The young boy pulled on his grandmother's arm. "Come on Grandma, let's go, who wants to buy anything from this dumb store anyway."

"You're absolutely right my boy." she glared at Adriana. "You have just made yourself one hell of an enemy. I hope you are ready for the consequences."

Even though Adriana was shaking inside, she stood her ground and held the door open. The woman stepped out onto the sidewalk followed by the young boy. "Thank you for your custom. Please feel free to never come back again."

"The cheek of it" the woman mumbled as she stomped up the street. "You'll be sorry."

"Yeah I already am. Sorry I ever let you enter my store."


Adriana was still shaking by the time she locked up the store and got into her car. It was hard to believe that in this day and age, there were still people like that around. That sort of behaviour was so archaic. Who did that woman think she was, expecting everyone to bow down to her? Parking the car in the driveway she hurried inside. "I'm sorry Mom," she called as she entered the house.

Patricia appeared from the kitchen. "Don't worry, they aren't here yet," she stopped dead. "What an earth is the matter with you, you look as if you've seen a ghost."

"Oh it's nothing really. Just a nasty old woman, who thinks she owns the town."

Patricia rolled her eyes, "Let me guess, Mrs April Radcliff."

Adriana's eye brows rose "how did you know?"

"Just about every person in this town has had a run in with her, some time or other. She's full of hot air. Don't take any notice of her."

Adriana's shoulders dropped as the tension left her body.

"Why does she have to be such a bitch all the time?"

Her mother shrugged, "Who knows. Maybe it's power or maybe it's something else. There is still no call for it."

"Hmmm..., she was pretty nasty, and she threatened me."

"Threatened you. Why?"

Adriana grinned, "For kicking her out of my store for one, and telling her to never come back."

Patricia's eyebrows shot up, "That's not like you."

"I know. She ticked me off."

They both laughed.

"We should be thankful we don't have to live with her."

A car horn sounded outside. Patricia grabbed her coat off the hook.

"Have a great time Mom."

"I will, and don't wait up. I might be late."

Adriana looked at her quizzically, "Is there something I

should know?"

Her mother smiled, "No, I just haven't been out in a while, so I'm going to make the most of it."

"Can I ask who you are going with?"

"I'm not sixteen."

"I know. I'm sorry. It comes from not having much of a social life. Go have fun."

"I will."

After her mother had left, Adriana stood looking at the closed door. It was about time her mother started going out again, she had spent far too much of time lately, looking after both of them. Over the last few days Adriana had been having feelings of her own, ones she wasn't quite sure what to do with.

"Mommy...," Madison called as she ran up the hall. Adriana crouched down and was nearly knocked off her feet when her daughter launched herself at her.

"I've been drawing," she grabbed Adriana's hand and began to pull her along the hall. As they entered the kitchen Adriana saw the paper and crayons were scattered across the table. Madison picked up the paper and waved it in front of her mother.

"Look Mommy. There's Daddy and Rick and you and me."

A lump caught in Adriana's throat. She had always made a point of telling Madison about her father and brother. There were photos of them in almost every room in the house, but it still hurt to see that her daughter was missing out. They had been living with her mother for two years now, and she still felt she wasn't quite ready for them be on their own. Their house. The one they had shared as a family was now being lived in by her sister and husband and their two children. She doubted she would ever have the strength to go back there. Her hand slipped around her daughters shoulder.

"That's really beautiful darling. What's this?" Adriana asked, pointing to a little yellow scribble in the corner of the page.

Madi looked up at her.

"It's a dog silly."

Adriana smiled, "But we don't have a dog."

Madi giggled. "Can we have a puppy, mommy? He could be my friend."

Tears threatened, she blinked them away quickly. Madi would have had a brother, if I hadn't insisted Alistair take Ricky out on that damn boat. Why hadn't she listened to her husband when he had tried to tell her that the weather wasn't ideal? At the time she had thought it was just another one of his many excuses. Her hand ruffled Madison's hair.

"I think it might be your bed time. How about you tidy up your things and I'll tuck you in and read you a bed time story?

Madison's eyes brightened, "Can you read Cinderella?"

Adriana sighed, "I suppose so, but it would be nice if you could pick a different one sometimes."

Madison looked up at her mother, "but I like Cinderella."

Adriana leant down and kissed the top of her head, "I know baby, I'm sorry, Cinderella it is."

Half an hour later as she pulled her daughter's door to, she found herself thinking about what Ross had said to her. As much as she hated to admit it, Ross was right, she needed to move on with her life. If not for herself, then for her daughter. They couldn't live here forever. Her husband had been a very competent sailor; he should have known it wouldn't have been safe. So why was she putting all the blame on herself? She walked along the hall to her room and sat down on the edge of the bed. Her eyes glistened as she glanced over at the photo of her husband and son which always stood on the dresser beside her bed. Picking it up, she rubbed her thumb across the glass. How did people move on from something like this? Guilt sat like a lead weight in the pit of her stomach. Tears trickled down her cheeks and dropped down onto the frame, she quickly wiped them away. Giving a long sigh she placed the frame back down on the dresser and lay back on the bed. How had the life that had once seemed so perfect. turned into such a mess? She closed her eyes. Maybe she should take up Ross's offer, she could do a lot worse. Shouldn't she at least give it a try? For Madi's sake. He would make a wonderful father, and maybe Madi would someday have another brother or sister. She shuddered at the thought. Turning over, she thumped the pillow. What was she thinking? There was no way she could be with Ross; it would feel wrong on so many levels. What she needed was to sort herself out, and she wasn't about to drag poor innocent Ross down to do it.

# Chapter Five

Why was it when you didn't want to see something, it always appeared at the most inopportune moments? Her face flushed as she brushed past him to enter the bank, ensuring to keep her head down hoping he wouldn't notice her.

"Hey. Hi there.,"

Reluctantly she turned to face him giving him the weakest of smiles.

"Hi" she replied, turning her attention on the man standing next to him.

"How are you?" he asked, forcing her to look at him. Another flush hit her cheeks. "I'm fine, thank you" she replied bluntly.

An awkward silence fell between them. Her attention returned to the other man. It was obvious they were related. He had the same blonde hair and piecing grey eyes. The man boldly stepped forward holding out his hand.

"Hi, I'm Jack."

She had little option but to take his hand. He squeezed it gently, holding onto it longer than necessary. Arrogance must run in the family she thought to herself, as she pulled her hand away.

Jack grinned, "Hayden, where have you been hiding this little beauty?"

Her eyes narrowed, "Excuse me, but no one has been hiding anyone."

Jack gave a sarcastic little laugh. This man was even more infuriating than the other one.

"Look, if you don't mind, I have to go," she began to move past them.

Hayden stiffened. Trust his brother to put his foot in it. "Right! Well goodbye..."

Not giving him a chance to finish she pushed past him and headed into the bank. He moved through the foyer, taking one last look back over his shoulder before stepping outside. His brother followed him out.

"So spill, who is she?"

Hayden gave him a cold stare, "none of your damn business, that's who."

"Oh come on bro," Jack said slapping Hayden on the shoulder. "You can tell me..., I must say she looks mighty fine. I wouldn't mind a bit of that myself."

Hayden spun on him, "You stay the hell away from her. Do you hear me?"

"Oh! So it's like that is it? Well I hate to tell you, but I don't think she even likes you." Hayden's brow creased, "We'll see," he muttered under his breath. He didn't give up that easily and was used to getting what he wanted, and she wouldn't be any different.

She had forgotten how good looking he was and what his smile could do to her.

"Excuse me."

Adriana turned to see the woman behind the counter staring at her impatiently.

Adriana walked up to the counter. "Sorry."

The woman smiled, "I can't blame you."

Adriana's brow creased, "Excuse me?"

The woman nodded towards the door, "The two that just left. I can't really blame you for getting a little distracted. Do you know them?"

Adriana felt her face heat, "No not really. Believe me they are not worth the bother."

The lady smiled a knowing smile, "R...ight."

Adriana's mood darkened as she quickly finished her transaction and left. Was she really that transparent? Could he see what he did to her?

The next day Adriana locked her store, and took a quick stroll along to her favourite coffee store. When she entered, there was a small queue and she joined it. The coffee here was well worth the wait. The door opened and she felt someone join the queue behind her. Whoever it was made a point of standing very close to her. She moved forward a little. The person behind her closed the gap.

"We are going to have to stop meeting like this." Her breath caught in her throat. He was so close she could smell his pine laced scent.

"Don't I even get a hello?"

Her cheeks flushed as she turned to face him. A smile touched his lips. Feeling a little overwhelmed, she took a step backwards, bumping into the lady behind her. Her blush deepened as she turned to apologize.

"I'm so sorry" she offered.

The woman turned to glare at her, "So I should thi.... Suddenly, the woman's face broke into a smile as she spied Hayden standing behind Adriana. "It's fine, really, no harm done" she said, all the while staring unashamedly up at Hayden.

Adriana rolled her eyes; she was right. Women did just fall at his feet. First it was the bank lady and now this woman. Her eyes narrowed as she turned back to him. "Are you following me?"

He grinned, "Would you mind if I was?"

Her heart gave a little flutter. "Of course I would. I'm not in the habit of being stalked."

His eyes twinkled, "So I'm a stalker now?" he gave a cynical little laugh. "So please tell me, why would I need to resort to stalking? When according to you, women fall at my feet," he said deliberately, looking up and giving the girl behind the counter a deviously charming smile.

Adriana sighed, "So why is it that I've never seen you here before?"

He was getting to her, he could see it. "Maybe you just didn't care to notice me before."

She opened her mouth to object, then thought better of it. He was probably right. Lately she had made a point of not making eye contact with men, especially good looking ones. A smile touched her lips "You're right, I would never have been interested in a man like you."

His gaze held hers, she felt her knees suddenly weaken. He grinned, "And... now?"

Adriana blinked up at him, "And now..., I'm... still not interested."

He laughed, causing her heart to race, "So why don't I believe you?"

"You can believe what you like, it's the truth."

"Hmm, so you say."

She stared up at him blankly.

He grinned, "It's your turn."

Her brow creased, "My turn for what?"

He pointed to the counter, "You're up."

Her face reddened as she turned, and walked up to the counter, "One cappuccino to go, please." She drew in a sharp breath as she felt him move in behind her. Her body stiffened as his warm breath brushed up the side of the neck. The woman took her money, all the while smiling up at Hayden.

Giving a long sigh, Adriana turned and pushed past him quickly making her way towards the door.

"Hey..., you never told me your name."

A smile touched her lips as she exited the store. He was charming when he wanted to be. If only her body would stop betraying her. Whenever she spent even a moment's time in his company she felt a little piece of her resistance being chipped away. No matter how hard she tried to pretend she didn't like him, he had an arrogant charm that was slowly breaking through her barriers. As much as she looked forward to their little encounters, she still wasn't quite ready to admit that she felt something for him.

On the last day of her working week, the bell on the  door tinkled. She looked up to see him entering her store. He was looking gorgeous as always. In a faded pair of jeans and a collared shirt open at the neck. His blonde hair was loosely tussled and a faint stubble lined his jaw. "Good morning," he said, giving her one of his dazzling smiles as he made his way to the counter with his casual lengthy stride. It took her a minute to compose herself as she struggled to remain calm. She felt the pink tinge creeping onto her cheeks. This was the first time they had been alone since the beach incident. It was unnerving to be with him in such a confined space.

"So, to what do I owe the pleasure?" her blush deepened, when she saw his eyes darken. Stupid, she thought to herself, why did she have to go and use the word pleasure?

"I'm in the market for something exciting for my bedroom."

Her eyes widened, "I don't think..."

He grinned, "A painting perhaps."

"Oh right..., did you have anything in mind?"

His eyes locked with hers, "something, sensual and sexy."

Her heart skipped a beat. He moved closer. Her body tensed, as the familiar smell of freshly cut pine drifted off his skin.

"Umm...," she moved over to a painting that she was sure he would like. It was of a woman draped across a bed. A thin piece of cloth covered her body, but her naked form was clearly visible beneath. He stood studying it for a few minutes rubbing his fingers across his chin. "Nice..., but not quite what I was looking for." His eyes turned to hers Looking away, she quickly moved on showing him several more paintings which he again rejected. Was he purposely trying to make her feel uncomfortable, she thought, moving to the next one. He stepped back to take in the full impact of the painting, he glanced from the painting to her, several times. It was then that she noticed the uncanny likeness between her and the figure in the painting. It was of a dark haired woman standing at the window, looking out at the ocean. Her dark hair fell around her shoulders just as hers did. The soft light from the window silhouetted her naked form. He smiled. "I'll take it."

When she turned to look at him she found him staring unabashedly at her. She shifted uncomfortably under his bold stare.

"Would you like it delivered or are you going to take it now?"

He smiled, "Delivered. You know where I live."

She moved behind the counter, glad to have something between them. He took out a wad of folded notes and counted some off. Again his eyes sought hers.

"Thank you for being so patient. I think it will look nice hanging on the wall above my bed."

Her eyes dropped to the counter. He handed her the money.

"Keep the change."

"That's not necessary."

His eyes darkened, "I won't take no for an answer."

She knew there was little point in arguing with him. All she wanted now, was him out of her store. "Can I at least have your name?"

His eyebrows rose.

Her palms began to sweat, "For the delivery."

He stood silently watching her, "Hayden." Then with a quick smile he turned and left the shop.

She blew out a long deep breath. Her eyes moved to the painting. Had he chosen it just to make her feel uncomfortable? Surely not. It was one of the most expensive paintings in the store. Slowly she began counting out the notes, she stiffened. He had paid her three hundred dollars too much. Her eyes turned to the door, had he done it deliberately? There was no way she could know. Should she simply keep it? Deciding that returning it was the right thing to do, she slipped the extra three hundred into her pocket, then put the rest in the till. He obviously must have miscounted. Nobody in their right mind gives away three hundred dollars.

# Chapter six

The next day she  found herself standing on the path  that led up to his house, trying to convince herself that the money was the only reason she was there. Over the past few days she had been unable to get him off her mind. Why was he so determined to make his presence known? The shells crunched under her feet as she slowly made her way up the path. As she neared the house, she was again struck by the peace and tranquillity surrounding her. The house stood in silence. Her palms began to sweat. What was she doing? Why had she come? Spinning on her heels she hurried back down the path, picking up her pace as she went. She was almost at a run by the time she hit the sand. A startled gasp escaped her lips when he jogged up beside her. She abruptly stopped, and he shot past a little way. He walked back to her.

Her eyes narrowed, "You scared the living daylights out of me."

He frowned, "If you had come up, I wouldn't have had to chase you halfway down the bay.

She dropped her eyes to the ground, "I... I thought you weren't home."

"So you were coming to see me?"

Her hands clasped together as she raised her eyes to meet his, "No I wasn't...."

His eyebrows rose.

"Okay fine..., I was."

"See, that wasn't so hard was it ?" he said, giving her one of his easy grins.

"Don't go getting any ideas," she pulled the notes from her pocket. "I just came to return this. You must have made a mistake and miscounted or something."

His face hardened, "No mistake."

"But I couldn't possibly..., it's too much."

His hand closed over hers, "Yes you can."

"I couldn't poss..."

"You will," he said with a bitter note rising in his voice. Giving an exasperated sigh she stuffed the notes back into her pocket, "Fine..., thank you."

"Good," he replied, watching her intently. "So you walked all the way down here just to return my money?"

"Y...yes." She tilted her chin up slightly, "Why else would I be here?"

"Hmm.., why else indeed? Why not simply wrap the money in with the painting ? Which looks great on the wall of my bedroom by the way. Would you like to see it?"

"NO!..., umm..., maybe another time." Her fingers intertwined with each other, "I thought it best if I delivered it in person just in case it got stolen, or lost." His eyes met hers, "I wouldn't have been any the wiser either way."

Her stomach clenched, "I wasn't to know that was I? What if you had realised your mistake; that would make me no more better than a thief."

"A very pretty thief."

Her cheeks heated, "I... have to go." She spun around and began to make her way back along the beach. Much to her annoyance he followed, keeping up easily with his long lengthy strides. "What's your hurry?"

"I have to get home," she focused her attention at the other end of the bay.

He reached out and grabbed hold of her arm, nearly pulling her off her feet as he spun her around to face him. "That's a lie and you know it."

She couldn't help but notice the coldness in his eyes. "And you would know that, how exactly ?" she replied glancing down to where his hand forcefully gripped her arm.

He dropped his hand, "You know, you are making it almost impossible for me to get to know you."

"Have you ever considered that maybe I don't want you to get to know me?"

His eyes softened, " No..., if I thought for one second that there was any hint of truth in what you just said I wouldn't be here."

"You don't even know me. How can you stand there and assume to know what I'm thinking?" she snapped. Her hand rose to clasp the locket secured around her neck. He glanced down at her hand.

"I know more about you than you realise."

"Oh! You do, do you..., so enlighten me."

His head nodded towards the locket, "Your husband and son, I take it."

Her grip tightened, "Who told you?"

He grinned, "You just did."

"It's none of your business."

"I agree."

The tension in her body eased, "You do?"

"Yes..., and I also owe you an apology."

Her eyebrows rose, "Why..., for being such a rude arrogant pig ?"

His eyes met hers, "Well, there is that..."

She gave a hint of a smile, "An apology. You know that's a very rare trait in a man?"

"Will you just let me finish?"

"By all means."

"That first day on the beach... I may have hinted... Okay, strongly suggested, that you had tried to drown yourself. I was wrong and I'm sorry."

Her heart clenched, "So what makes you so sure I wasn't?"

He smiled, her stomach did a little somersault. "I saw how much you love your daughter." Tears pricked the backs of her eyes.

"Thank you."

A single tear trickled down her cheek. He reached out and brushed it away.

"Don't...please!" she replied, stifling a sob.

His brow creased, "Give me one good reason why not."

"Because I don't want you to. Isn't that enough?"

He let out a sigh, holding up his hands in defeat. "Fine... whatever you want, but just answer me this. How long are you going to use your husband and son's deaths as an excuse to hide from the world?"

Her fists bunched into tight balls, "I'm not hiding, and for your information it's called respect. I loved them and always will. But I can't expect someone like you to understand that."

His voice softened "I'm not disputing your love for them. Anyone can see you are still hurting. Tell me what happened."

Her eyes were rimmed with tears, she hadn't spoken to anyone about the accident, not since the day they had called off the search. So why now, did she feel the urge to tell a man she had only just met? She swallowed, "They drowned! Okay, so there, now you know."

He stood silently watching her.

"Have you heard enough?" Her chest heaved. Still he didn't answer. Tears flooded her cheeks. He didn't move to comfort her.

She glanced up at him with her tear stained face. "It was my fault. I sent them out there... They never came back. That was two years ago. They are lost out there forever." She swiped at her tears. "There, so is that a good enough reason for you?" Her eyes fell to her feet. Silence filled the air. She began to scrape her foot back and forth across the sand, her body rigid with tension. He took hold of her chin and tipped her head up.

She glanced up at him with tear soaked lashes. "What do you want from me?"

He remained silent, assessing her with his eyes.

"I have nothing to give," she sobbed.

His look intensified as he brushed his thumb gently across her quivering lips.

"You're wrong." He smiled. "You've just forgotten how." Her eyes closed, savouring his touch. A feeling of guilt washed over her and she pulled away. "Don't! Please..., I can't do this. I won't betray him."

She turned to leave.

He grabbed her arm in a tight vicelike grip "He wouldn't want you to do this. He would want you to be happy."

"Happy," she gave a snort, "I have lost my family and you think I should be happy. What do you know about anything.?"

"I'm sure he never intended for you to be staring out at the ocean day after day, mourning him as your own life slowly ticks by."

Her anger flared, "And how could you possibly know what he would have wanted?"

He glanced at her soft trembling lips. Suddenly he pulled her into his arms, lowering his lips to hers. Kissing her with a sudden urgency that she had neither the strength, nor desire to resist. She found herself responding, desperately wanting to be touched. Parting her lips she allowed his tongue to explore the softness of her mouth. A small moan escaped as she slipped into a moment of unchecked wanting. He pulled away. Her eyes widened; instantly her mind began to swim with thoughts of betrayal and guilt. Placing her hand against his chest she tried to push him away, but he wasn't quite ready to let her go.

Her eyes narrowed "Why! Did you do that?"

He looked down into her eyes, his still dark with wanting, "I wanted to show you that you do have something to give. Life is there to be lived."

Her eyes turned to the ocean, "I can't, won't let them go."

He sighed "If I loved a woman as much as your husband obviously loved you, I wouldn't want her to be wasting her life mourning me."

She tried to pull away, what he had said was true, but she wasn't ready, not yet. Her eyes moistened, "Please, let me go."

His grip remained fast, "I'm sorry. I didn't mean to upset you, but I felt you needed someone to point out the obvious."

Her heart welled with emotion "Well! Thanks very much! I feel much better now. With one kiss you've fixed everything," she spat sarcastically 'Now will you kindly let go of me ?"

He hesitated, knowing he couldn't let her go, not like this. "I'll let you go on one condition."

Anger flared in her eyes. "What! What do you want from me now?"

He smiled, "Your name."

She hesitated. "Why?"

"Because I just kissed you and I still don't know your name."

Her lips twitched, but she wasn't going to give him the satisfaction of seeing her smile, "Adriana, now please let me go."

He released his hold, "Well Adriana, it was a pleasure to meet you."

# Chapter Seven

Now that he had let her go, she wasn't sure she wanted to leave. Glancing up at him, she realised he was too dangerous for her to be around. Her body gave a quick quiver. His kiss had stirred something in her; something forbidden. Alistair had always been quiet and softly spoken, caring and attentive. There were very little of those qualities in the man who stood before her. He had a sullen strength about him that commanded respect. His eyes were cold and calculating. Yet she had seen something in them when he had kissed her, that made her body quiver with anticipation. Granted his personality certainly had some irritating flaws, but that was all part of the attraction. You never knew where you stood with him or what he would do next.

His cool grey eyes scanned her face. He wasn't sure what it was about her that had him constantly thinking about her.

She stared up at him, her long dark lashes blinking slowly across her beautiful green eyes. What did he want from her? As the seconds ticked by she began to doubt her reasons for coming. There was no way she could let this go any further.

"Look, I really should be going," she hesitated. Then for reasons unbeknown to her, she reached out and gently brushed her fingers down his cheek and along his strong defined jaw line. His sharp intake of breath took her by surprise. Quickly withdrawing her hand she turned to leave. He caught her wrist in his hand. Her eyes widened, as found herself drawn against him. She struggled, pushing firmly against his chest. He held her fast. The heat of his body radiating through his shirt. His taut muscles moved beneath her fingers as he fought to retain his grip. His hand slipped up the back of her neck and into her hair. He took a firm grip and pulled her head back, that so she had no choice but to look up into his grey volatile eyes. A small quiver ran up her spine as his eyes held her captive.

"Don't say you don't feel it, because I know you do" he said, his voice now deep and raspy.

Shocked at her inability to deny it, she nodded. He tugged on her hair, drawing her head back to expose the soft pale flesh of her neck. His lips brushed lightly up the side of her throat. A soft moan escaped her lips. Had it really been that long since she had felt the touch of a man? Two years without so much as a kiss. His lips were warm against her highly sensitised skin. His kisses were growing more urgent as he devoured her exposed flesh. Her eyes closed, as powerful sensations of wanting washed over her. How could she be doing this with a man that she hardly knew? It was obvious that he was the type of man who was used to getting what he wanted. Would he simply discard her when he had had his fill? Her breathing quickened, as he slid his free hand down over her back, and onto her buttocks, pulling her against him. At this precise moment she didn't care to think about it, as the urgency of his need quickly became apparent. A moistness seeped between her legs, as her arousal rose to match his. His lips reached the soft crest of her breast peeking above her shirt. Her hands slipped up into his hair, she felt him smile against her skin. If there had been a time when she should have felt embarrassed at her wanton behaviour, it had passed. Now caught up in the whirlpool of sensations flowing throughout her body all thoughts of her husband had momentarily vanished. She was powerless to deny herself the one thing she had secretly dreamed of since the first day she had met him. He popped the top two buttons of her shirt, and pushed it back to expose her lace covered breasts. Her soft pink nipples, pushed teasingly outwards in hard little peaks against the lace. He lowered his head and sucked one into his mouth. If he carried on like this, she would reach her peak in a matter of minutes.

"Please...."

He released her nipple, "What is it you want, tell me?"

Her face flushed," I want..., you...."

He ground himself against her, "You want me where?"

Her cheeks glowed pink, "Inside me," she murmured.

He wouldn't have any trouble obliging and it wasn't that he normally felt the need to ask twice. But for some reason he found himself hesitating.

"Adriana, look at me."

She glanced up at him through her thick lashes.

He gave a small groan, "Are you sure about this..., I think we should... "

"Please, don't think. I need this." she said, grabbing for the buttons on his shirt.

He let out a long groan. He was going to regret this, he was sure of it. Sweeping her up into his arms he made his way to a bushy area just off the beach. He was now just as powerless to stop as she was. Since he had first laid eyes on her it was all he ever thought about. They fell to the ground, their kisses now frantic and hungry. Making short work of his shirt, she tossed it aside as her hands now greedily roamed his chest and down across his hard flat abdomen. He tore at the front of her shirt, causing the remaining buttons to pop off. He pushed it back off her shoulders. She lifted up as he dragged it from her body and took the opportunity to capture one of her nipples in his mouth. Her back arched, accentuating the long lean lines of her body. Reaching around her he unclipped her bra and drew it down her arms, tossing it on the ground. He feasted his eyes on her soft pale flesh, cupping a breast in his hand. She gave a little groan as he gently rolled her nipples between his fingers, lightly flicking the tips with his tongue. He was now rock hard with need and wanted nothing more than to totally possess her. She gave a little shiver as the cool sea breeze skimmed across her body, causing small bumps to appear across the surface of her skin. He moved his hands over her body in a way that only came from experience. Intense heat radiated from her core, as an insistent throbbing began to build between her legs. The pain of her loss had long since left her as he explored every inch of her body. He slid his hands up her legs, pushing her skirt up around her hips. His fingers hooked into her lacy underwear. He dragged them down and flung them away. She was ready for him and the thought made him harden even more. Frantically, she began to fumble with the button on his pants. He stilled her hands. Her face heated as he began undoing the zip on his pants. His eyes held hers as he pushed his jeans down over his hips. Surprised at the powerful need growing inside him. He slipped his boxers down and saw only raw desire as her eyes feasted on his male hardness. Pushing her legs apart his eyes took in her swollen womanly folds. He positioned himself between her parted legs pressing his engorged tip against her, gently nudging at her opening. Her eyes closed, "Now" she pleaded.

He thrust into her. Letting out a loud groan she raised her pelvis to meet him. Again and again he drove into her, she clutched at him, lost to the world around her. Suddenly her pelvis bucked upwards as her body flew into one of the most powerful climaxes she had ever experienced in her life. Her thighs clamped around him as she cried out into the wind. A long deep groan escaped his lips as he drove himself in even deeper and he exploded inside her. Holding nothing back he gripped her hips, holding her firmly as his body released itself.

Completely spent, he let his body relax down onto hers. Their hearts raced in unison. He closed his eyes. He had never imagined it would be like this. It wasn't how he had envisaged their first time together. What was it about this woman that made him lose all self control and give himself to her so totally? She moved beneath him. He rose up on his elbows and looked down into a face full of regret. In that exact instant he knew had made a terrible mistake.

"Get off me," she hissed.

He rolled to one side and she quickly scrambled away from him.

"No..., oh no. What have you done?"

He looked over at her.

"Don't look at me," she spat, stifling a sob as she snatched her shirt from the ground and held it in front of her. He slapped his hand to his forehead and let out a long agonised groan.

Her eyes narrowed.

"What!  This is your fault. Why couldn't you just leave me alone?"

He gave a cynical little laugh "Excuse me!" You were the one that came out here, and if my memory serves me right, I'm sure I heard you say..., oh' what was it again?" He grinned, "I want you inside me."

She gasped as a deep flush flooded her cheeks "You knew

how vulnerable I was. You took advantage of me." As she scrambled to collect her clothes, he lay there making no attempt to move.

His brow creased, "I'm not in the habit of forcing myself on anybody."

Snatching her bra from the ground she turned her back to him and put it on. She slipped on her shirt, doing up the two remaining buttons. He lay there staring at her. She drew her shirt around her clutching it against her chest. He got to his feet. She quickly turned away pretending to brush the creases from her skirt. He slipped into his jeans as her eyes scored the ground for her underwear. He plucked them from the ground, hooking them on one finger. "Are you looking for these by any chance?"

Her cheeks coloured. "Give them to me."

He gave a smug grin. "I'll give them to you in return for a kiss."

There was no way she was going to risk going anywhere near him. A little quiver ran up her spine. The sensations he had awoken in her brought another deep flush to her cheeks. The temptation to fall back into his arms was too strong. Her back stiffened. She had betrayed her husband's memory for what? A quick romp in the bushes with a complete stranger. The guilt began to weigh down heavily on her. He swung her panties around on one finger. "So, do you want them or not?"

Her fists clenched as she gave him a cold stare. "Keep them as a memento of our one and only time together," she hissed. Jamming her hand into her pocket she drew out the small fold of notes and tossed them at him. "And

you can keep this. I don't want your damn money."
He stood watching as she turned and ran down the beach. The wind caught the money and it scattered across the sand. It was obvious there was no point in going after her. The state she was in, there would be no way she would see reason. His brow creased hoping he would get a chance to put things right. Stuffing her underwear into his back pocket, he headed home. She was stubborn. The corner of his lip twitched, but she would come around..., eventually he would make sure of it.

Holding her skirt down with one hand whilst gripping her shirt tightly with the other she quickly made her way home. A sob escaped her lips, knowing she must look a sight. What had possessed her to go out there when all her instincts had told her to stay well away? Her body quivered as she recalled the touch of his fingers on her skin, the taut muscular lines of his body. The feel of his hot kisses. How was she ever supposed to go back to her life and forget him? She shook her head and groaned. This wasn't getting her anywhere.

"Stupid," she mumbled as she climbed the steps to her mother's house. Closing the front door quietly she snuck up to her room unnoticed. Shutting herself in her room, she walked straight into the bathroom and flicked on the shower. Then just as quickly turned it off, not wanting to wash the smell of him off her skin. Giving a loud sob, she threw herself down on the bed. What had she done? Never in her life had she experienced anything so powerful. Turning on her side, she curled herself up into a ball, clutching her arms around her body as she let the tears fall.  A heavy feeling of guilt settled over her. Part of her wanted nothing more than to honour the promise she had made to herself, but it was no longer that simple. Today had awoken something in her. There was a life out there waiting for her. For the first time in two years she felt the need to move on. Her arms tightened around her body. She had loved her husband with all her heart and still did. However there was no denying the feelings she now had for Hayden, a man who had just woken a need in her. One that she had tried so hard to bury.

There was a soft tap at the door. Adriana sat up quickly wiping away the tears "What."
"It's me, I was just wondering if you're okay."
"I'm fine Mom. I've just got a bit of headache. I'll be down shortly. I'm just going to take a quick shower."
"Okay..., as long as you're sure,"
"I'm sure."
Her mother left. She got up off the bed and went into the bathroom and turned on the shower. As her clothes dropped to the floor her reflection stared back at her from the mirror. Her hands moved up her body to gently caress her breasts. Closing her eyes, she could almost feel his hand and lips on her body. Her nipples instantly hardened. Her hands dropped to her sides. What had he done to her? The Adriana she had known would never have done what she just did.

Hayden slipped his hands behind his head.

Leaning back in the chair, he gazed out over the ocean. It was hard to believe that he had just had the most amazing sex he had ever had in his life. What he didn't understand was, why her? His brow creased, he hoped he hadn't blown it with her. It wasn't in him to leave things the way they were, even if she had insisted that was what she wanted. Why hadn't he listened to that little voice in the back of his head, telling him to stop? A smiled played at the corners of his mouth. He had acted like a young boy instead of an experienced man. The plan had been to seduce her and earn her trust. He pushed his fingers through his hair. The blame certainly didn't lie with her. It would be his own damn fault if she never wanted to see him again. He had tried to convince himself that the outcome didn't matter but to no avail. Was she to be another casualty to be added to the so called list she had insisted he had? If it had been simply for the sex, it would have made things a whole lot simpler. No matter what she thought, there was no list and no belt to add notches to. He had always been rather selective about whom he slept with and of late his high expectations had left him very short of bed companions. He wasn't in the habit of having sex with random woman. He smiled, well not until today anyway. Never before had he ever experienced such a strong attraction to anyone. A deep ache settled inside him. How had he managed to become so totally obsessed with this woman in such a short space of time?

# Chapter Eight

Adriana tried hard to forget what had taken place out at the beach that day, and was in some way thankful that he hadn't tried to see her again. Her chest tightened; he had got what he wanted. It was obvious that she was just another notch in his belt. Well that suited her just fine, her loyalties lay elsewhere and she wouldn't let herself slip up again. He had willingly obliged, meeting her needs, now she was ready to move on. What had happened didn't change a thing. She still loved her husband and would honour his memory forever.

Hayden lay on his back, his arms tucked behind his head, his long muscular legs stretched out down the length of the bed. He had been unable to stop thinking about her. What was with him lately? In the past he had always found it so easy to push women away. Granted, the fact that most of them had been forced onto him by his mother made it easier to reject them. Maybe that was the attraction. She seemed to have no knowledge of who he was, or how much money he had. Being attracted to a woman who was a mother of a three year old wasn't exactly what he considered ideal. He smiled, his mother certainly wouldn't approve. The child however was a factor that bothered him. He wasn't really father material and wasn't even sure if he wanted children, let alone another man's child. His brother had already taken care of a  grandson for his mother, so why subject another child to a woman who didn't even understand what the words, 'family', 'unity' or 'love' meant. Both his parents had been more  interested in making money than in their children.

He pushed his hands through his hair. He needed to see her and sort this out, one way or another. The deep ache that had formed in the pit of his stomach hadn't left him as he had thought it would. The easy option would be to simply walk away. Hadn't she already been through enough? There was more at stake than his own selfish needs. He gave an exasperated sigh, as he got up off the bed and pulled his clothes on. If he didn't make an effort to get to the office soon, he would have his mother breathing down his neck. He glanced over at the lace underwear sitting on his dresser and smiled. Snatching the receiver out of the phone cradle, he punched in a number on the speed dial.

"Hello, Stevenson's Florist, how can I help you?"
He cringed at the sound of her voice, "Hi..., it's Hayden."
"Oh, hi," she replied her voice turning silky smooth, "how are you?"
"Fine thanks and you?" He gripped the phone in frustration but kept his voice calm.
"Oh I'm good, it's nice to hear from you" she purred seductively.
He wanted to move it along. Not wanting to give her any reason to think he was still interested in her. "Look I'm in a bit of a hurry. I would like to place an order for two dozen red roses and could you put some of those white lilies in the centre?"
The line went quiet.
"Jessica... Are you still there?"
"Of course I'm still here. Where would you like them sent" she snapped down the phone.
"Twenty one Elbridge Lane."
"And what do you want the card to say?" she asked bitterly.
"Oh..., of course," he heard her sigh. He hesitated, what was it he wanted to say?
He relayed a short message.
"Right then, when would you like them delivered."
He rolled his eyes, "Today, as soon as possible."
"Fine, I have your details. I'll send you the bill, will that be all?"
"Yes and..., thanks" he replied to an empty line. So she was still upset with him. His mother certainly had a lot to answer for. He could understand her being a little hurt. He

had been quite blunt with her in the end but she just wouldn't take no for an answer. If there had been another decent florist in town he wouldn't have risked ringing. But with his mother's help, Jessica had managed to wipe out the only competition in town. He walked through the door and out onto the balcony. The sun glistened off the water. He took a deep breath of sea air, rolling his shoulders trying to ease some of the tension. If his mother carried on the way she was, there wouldn't be a eligible female left in town who  hadn't been placed in front of him at some time or other. He gave a heavy sigh and headed back inside.

He ambled into the boardroom half an hour late. Everyone was already seated and waiting. Acknowledging everyone with a curt nod, he placed the customary kiss on his mother's cheek and took his seat.

"Sorry I'm late."

His mother eyed him suspiciously. He had never been late in his life. His mother's face twisted in disgust when she noticed the shadow across his chin and jaw line. "What's the matter with you boy, you look like you slept under a bush. Couldn't you have at least had the decency to shave?"

Every pair of eyes turned on him.

He gave his mother a forced smile, "Can we just get on with this?"

April gave an impatient 'humph' then turned her attention back to the other board members. Glancing around the room, he began to wonder why he had bothered. Everyone sat looking at his mother expectantly. Both  his brothers were sitting opposite him. Jack was the eldest by two years. At twenty Ethan was the baby of the family. Hayden glanced across at his three sisters, Mary and Alice were identical twins, he smiled; and second in line for the throne. Janice caught his attention and crossed her eyes. He struggled to stifle a smile. Janice was the only one he ever spent any time with outside of work. She was younger than him by two years and he had always felt the need to protect her. As children they would disappear together to explore the coast. Neither of their parents ever really missed them. The nanny used to scold them, with a smile on her face. She understood only too well the need for them to escape the stifling confines of the dreary lifeless household. He glanced across at his uncle. Tobias had joined the company just after his  father had died. His eyes moved between his uncle and his mother. He had always felt there was something more between them. These days they never seemed to be apart. Not that he would care. He wasn't really interested in anything his mother did outside of the business. To the right of his mother sat the meek and mild mannered Alex, the family accountant. Hayden felt someone's eyes on him; he turned to find Jack staring at him. Jack gave Hayden one of his stupid lop sided grins.

"Have a hard night did we?"

Hayden's eyes narrowed, the grin dropped from Jack's face.

"Geez, if looks could kill, I'd be lying stone cold dead right now."

April thumped her fist down on the table, "What the hell is going on? We're in the middle of a meeting if you hadn't noticed."

Her cold hard stare fell on Hayden, "Which is now running late thanks to you... Is there anything either of you would like to share?" she asked glaring at each of them in turn.

"No," snapped Hayden glaring at his brother.

"Good, then let's continue, hopefully with no more interruptions."

Hayden was so over these boring meetings. Down on the floor with the workers was where he preferred to be, keeping his finger on the pulse. And hopefully one step ahead of any possible problems. A breakdown could cost them hundreds of thousands of dollars for every hour the machines were down. A smile touched his lips. Since he had been in charge of the mill there had been no breakdowns and productivity was up by thirty percent. His mother had no interest in the day to day running of the mill. All she ever worried about was making money. No matter how unethical it was. His mind began to drift, the room's proceedings fell to a dull murmur as he again found himself thinking about Adriana.

"Hayden! What an earth is the matter with you today...," his mother gave an exasperated sigh. "Hayden!" she screamed.

He slowly turned to look at her. Her lips drew into a thin line as she fixed him with one of her cold hard stares. He almost laughed. Did she really think she could intimidate him?

"What is with you today? First you arrive late and look like you have just fallen out of bed, and now your mind is off somewhere  else. You may as well not even be here. You certainly haven't contributed anything useful." Surprising even himself, he shoved his chair back and rose to his feet.

"You know what, Mother, you are absolutely right." Mouths dropped open as he made his way to the door. His mother got to her feet.

"Hayden Radcliff, you come back here this minute".

He ignored her and kept walking.

"I mean it Hayden..., Hayden!"

No one ever went against his mother. It had been that way ever since his father had passed away eight years ago, but today for some reason he didn't care. He strode out of the room pulling the door closed behind him. A smile touched his lips as he imagined the look on his mother's face. He pushed the down arrow on the wall and waited for the elevator to arrive. The board room door opened. He didn't bother turning around.

"Hayden, you get back in here this instant," his mother screeched across the office.

The receptionist at the front desk sat staring open mouthed. She had never seen anyone of the family go against their mother's wishes. He winked at her giving a slight grin.

"Hayden, you will be sorry for this."

The elevator pinged and the doors opened, he stepped inside. It was only then that he turned to face his mother. He smiled at her as the doors slowly closed. He could still hear her yelling as the lift descended down through the floors. He felt sorry for everyone else left in that room. They were certainly going to cop an earful today. When the elevator reached the basement he stepped off. It had felt good to finally assert himself. They had all tiptoed around her for far too long. Grinning widely he strode over to his truck, unlocked it and slipped behind the wheel. What was his mother going to think when he didn't turn up tomorrow? His brow creased. He had better ring Jack later, and warn him. On second thoughts, they all needed to learn to stand up to her.

# Chapter Nine

Adriana was finding it hard to focus as she dusted the same spot for the third time. The store had been unusually quiet for the last two days and it was beginning to worry her. It wasn't as though she was struggling, but too many days without sales didn't look good for her clients. The phone rang, startling her. She reached over and picked it up.

"Hello, Madison's handcrafts. Adriana speaking."

"Oh..., hi, Adriana. It's Leslie. How are you?"

Adriana picked up a pen and absently began writing his name, "Fine thank you, how's the family?"

"Everyone is good thanks. Listen, I hate to do this to you."

Adriana's pen stilled.

"But I need to finish out my contract at the end of the month."

Adriana's grip tightened on the phone, "Can I ask why?"

Leslie hesitated, "I'd rather not say. It's a personal matter."

The pen dropped out of her hand. "Nothing serious I hope?"

"Oh no, nothing like that."

The line went quiet.

"Well, if there is anything I can do to help don't hesitate to ask."

"No, no I'll be fine," Leslie replied, sounding a little uncomfortable.

"I'll pack your items at the end of the month and send you the bill for packaging and freight, unless you would prefer to pick them up."

There was silence on the other end. "Leslie, are you sure you are okay?"

"Oh! What,? Of course, look if you could just send them over to my home address that would be great."

"Leslie, it's not something I've done is it?"

There was another long strained silence. "No, of course not. You've been wonderful. It's just that I... I have to go out of town for a while. I'm not sure if I'll be back."

"Oh, right. Well, I'll miss you. Take care."

"I will. Goodbye Adriana and thanks for everything. It's been really great working with you."

"Thank you, and the same applies to you. If ever you find yourself in a position to need my services again, please don't hesitate to ask."

"I won't," The line went dead.

Adriana placed the phone back on the hook, her brow

creased. Why would Leslie feel the need to finish her contract? Over the last couple months she had managed to sell quite a few of her pieces. Even if she was leaving town she could still keep her art work here. It just didn't seem to make any sense.

Throughout the day she had two very similar calls from other loyal clients, wanting to finalise their accounts. None of them really gave her any reason for their sudden desire to end their contracts. By the end of the day she had lost three really good clients. Something else had to be going on. She hadn't lost a client since she had opened a year ago. Now all of a sudden she had lost three in one day. None of them had really wanted to tell her why. That, along with the store being unusually quiet, just didn't seem to add up.

By the time she closed up, her head was pounding. Pressing her fingers into her temples she tried to massage away the pain. As she locked the shop door she suddenly remembered the warning she had received. Her brow creased, as she tried to remember Mrs Radcliff's exact words. "You'll be sorry" Wasn't that what she had said?  Surely the woman wouldn't stoop so low as to put someone out of business over a minor altercation?

She was still  mulling over the possibility when she walked through the front door of her mother's house. The large bouquet of flowers dominating the front entrance didn't register at first. Closing the door, she let her handbag drop to the floor. The flower's perfume was a little overpowering in such a confined space. Her brow creased, they looked very expensive. At that very moment her mother came hurrying down the hall with a huge grin on her face.

"Aren't they beautiful? They came for you this afternoon."

Adriana sighed as she walked over and plucked the card from the bouquet. Her mother stood watching her as she opened it.

*Dear Adriana,*

*I'm sorry. I really didn't mean for things to get so out of hand. We need to talk. I'll be at Crofters Cafe at ten thirty tomorrow morning, please come.*

*Hayden.*

He was sorry; he damn well should be. So he had a conscience after all. Apology or not, there was no way she was going to put herself in that situation again. Tossing the card on the table she reached down and retrieved her handbag from the floor. It was a little too late for apologies.

"So..., who's it from?"

Adriana glanced over at her mother, "Nobody..., a client."

Her mother eyed her suspiciously, "So what's he sorry for."

Adriana's eyes widened, "you read it?"

Her mother gave her a tentative smile, "I'm sorry. I couldn't help myself. So who is he? This Hayden fellow."

"No one, I'm not even going to go."

Her mother's eyes fixed on hers, "Can I ask why not? He was nice enough to send you a beautiful, and very expensive bouquet of flowers. Don't you think you at least owe him a thank you?"

"Mom please. Just stay out of it. It's complicated."

"My dear girl, life is complicated, as you well know, but you still have to live it. Now I'm telling you as your mother, and someone that cares very deeply for you... you should go."

Adriana picked up the card and read it again. Maybe she should go and see what he had to say for himself. The corner of her lips twitched at the thought of seeing him again. But she wasn't quite ready to admit that he had already stolen  past her defences.

"So, are you going?"

Adriana gave her mother a forced smile, "Okay, I'll go, happy now."

Her mother smiled, "yes."

Adriana rolled her eyes. "Oh, and in the future, leave the card reading to me if you don't mind."

"I'll try." Adriana glared at her, "Okay, fine, no more card reading."

"Good, now I'm going upstairs for a minute," she said, as she discreetly slipped the card into her pocket.

Entering her room she closed the door behind her and sat down on the bed. Pulling the note out of her pocket, she read it again. Why did he want to see her? Hadn't he already managed to get what he wanted, and quite easily, she thought rather ashamedly. It would be unfair of her to lay all the blame at his feet. After all hadn't she virtually thrown herself at him? She flopped down on the bed. What on earth had possessed her to do such a thing, with a virtual stranger? Not that she didn't enjoy it or need it. The fact that she had responded to him so willingly still unsettled her. There was no way she was going to fall at his feet and risk making a complete fool of herself. Her eyes turned back to the note. What did he want from her and would she be willing to give it? Dropping the note on the dresser, she got up and walked over to the mirror to study her reflection. What did he want with a widow and a mother of a three year old, with a not quite so perfect body? Tears began to trickle down her cheeks, Why did he have to go and make things even more difficult with his romantic gesture of flowers? Beautiful, expensive flowers at that. There was a soft tap at the door. Adriana quickly wiped away her tears and went and sat back down on the bed.  "Come in." Patricia entered, noticing her daughter's damp lashes. "I'm sorry," she said walking over and placing a kiss on top of her daughters head, "I didn't mean to pry."

"It's okay Mom. Honestly. No harm done."

Her mother sat down on the bed beside her and slipped her arm around her daughter's waist, "I just want the best for my little girl."

"I know Mom, but I'm not your little girl anymore. I need to sort this out on my own."

Her mother gave her waist a little squeeze, "I know that love.... I just wish that you would let go of the guilt, and move on with your life. You deserve to be happy." Adriana's head snapped around, "Do I! Really...? And why's that Mom? It was my fault they were out there. If I hadn't been so damn stubborn, I'd be sitting here waiting for my loving husband to get home, enjoying the time with my son and daughter. A daughter, I might add, who is now growing up without a father or a brother because of me."

"Adriana! Stop it! It was an accident."

"An accident that I helped create."

"You can't blame yourself."

"Can't I? Well it's a bit late for that, because I already do. Mom, if you don't mind I'd like to be alone. I've had a rough day and I'm not in the mood for lectures."

Her mother made no effort to leave.

"Didn't you hear me, I asked you to leave." Tears sprung to Adriana's eyes, "Oh... Mom..., I can't do this. It's too hard. I wanted so much to be a good mother to Madison, and successful at the same time. But everything seems to be stacked against me."

Her mother patted her hand, "You put far too much pressure on yourself. When was the last time you actually had some fun?"

Adriana began sobbing uncontrollably. "Adriana, talk to me. Let me help you."

Adriana took a deep breath, "That's the thing Mom. Something good did happen..., something wonderful actually. But I don't deserve it."

Her mother raised her eyebrows, "Why didn't you tell me?"

"I feel so guilty."

Her mother's brow creased, "You have no reason to feel guilty."

Adriana turned to her mother, "I met a man."

"There see, it's not all bad. Good things can still happen."

Adriana looked at her mother, "Don't you see?"

Her mother stared blankly at her, "Apparently I don't, what are you trying to say."

Adriana sighed, "He's not like any other man I've ever met before."

"And that's a problem."

Adriana's shoulder's drooped "I can't let myself like him. I promised myself I wouldn't. And what about Madi? I have to consider her."

"So he doesn't like children. Is that it?"

"No..., oh shit. I don't know... I never had the chance to ask him." Adriana looked across at her mother, "I think I could really fall for him Mom, if I haven't already."

"And that's not a good thing?"

"No it's not, and you know only too well why. I don't deserve it. Anyway, what would he want with a woman like me when he could have almost any woman he desired?"

Her mother smiled and stood up drawing Adriana to her feet. She led her over to the mirror. "Take a good look Adriana. Do you want to know what I see?"

Adriana stared blankly at her own reflection.

Patricia smiled, "I see an intelligent, beautiful young

woman in the prime of her life. One who has the ability to love someone so deeply that it almost consumes her. You are a loving passionate woman who needs someone to love in her life. You are not complete without it, no matter how much you try to convince yourself you are."

"But I have love in my life. I have you and Madi. That's all I need."

"Oh Adriana if that were true, we wouldn't be having this conversation. You shouldn't feel guilty about falling in love. It's what helps make you complete."

"So you're saying I'm incomplete without a man, and that I can't possibly function without one?"

"No that's not what I'm saying and you know it. What I mean is you are content, happier, more fulfilled when you have a man in your life. Is that so bad? You can't tell me you didn't like it that a man showed interest in you. Don't try to deny it because I will know you are lying."

Adriana smiled, "You know Mom. Sometimes I think you know me better than myself."

"So, does that mean you will really think about what I just said?"

Adriana rolled her eyes and gave a little laugh as visions of what she had already done with him sprung to mind. "What's so funny?"

"Nothing, just a thought that's all. Thanks Mom. I desperately needed that pep talk." Adriana turned towards the bathroom. "I'm going to take a shower. Can you let Madi know I'll be down shortly?"

Her mother gave her hand a reassuring squeeze "Sure, take your time, dinner's going to be another half hour or so yet." Her mother turned to leave.

"Hey Mom. I meant to ask you. You know that customer I had the other day, the one who held me up that night and told me I'd be sorry?"

"Mrs Radcliff."

"That's the one. Do you think she would go as far as sabotaging my business?"

Patricia's eyes widened, "Why, has something happened?"

"Sort of..., that's why I thought I'd ask you. Do you think she would be capable of carrying out her threats?"

"Well I haven't heard of her ever doing so, but that's not to say she wouldn't. If she really wanted to, I guess she could. Why? What is it you think she has done?"

"Nothing, well nothing I can honestly say isn't coincidence. I suppose I'll just have to wait and see."

Her mother frowned, "What's happened?"

"I'll tell you later, it's probably nothing."

"Okay, as long as you're sure."

"Yes, I'm sure it's fine, just me over reacting. Go on down stairs and see to Madi, I'll be down soon."

Her mother gave her a sympathetic smile, then left.

Adriana stripped out of her clothes and stood in front of the mirror. Her fingers lightly traced the faint stretch marks that ran down her lower abdomen. A flaw in her otherwise perfectly smooth skin. Placing her hand over the scars she tried imagining herself without them. They had never really bothered her before. Her husband had never commented on them, but another man seeing her naked, that was a whole different story. She ran a critical eye over her body, taking in the changes to it since the birth of her beloved children. Her breasts were no longer as firm and perky as they had once been. They were still nicely rounded but now sat a little lower on her chest. Turning to the side she saw that her abdomen was no longer flat. She ran her hand over the soft roundedness of her flesh. For her age she was still in pretty good shape, but would she be good enough for the likes of him? He was in such pristine condition, what would he want with her, except for what she had already freely given him.

Half an hour later Adriana walked into the kitchen.

"Mommy," Madison yelled, launching herself at her mother. Adriana staggered backwards a little, just managing to retain her balance. She picked Madison up and gave her a tight hug, placing lots of little kisses on her face. Madison giggled.

"You know baby, you're going to have to stop doing that. You're getting too big to throw yourself at me."

"I've been waiting for you."

"I know baby. I'm sorry. Mommy had a hard day today, and needed a bit of time alone."

Madison pulled away from her, "Were you crying Mommy?"

Adriana smiled. "You certainly don't miss much do you? Yes maybe a little, but I'm fine now I promise."

"Did that man make you cry?"

Adriana glanced across at her mother, "No darling he didn't make me cry."

Later that night after Adriana had put her daughter to bed, she came back down to talk to her mother. "So what's with this woman?"
"As I said before, it's nothing I can confirm. But today I had three clients ring and cancel their contracts. I have never had anyone cancel. Now I've had three in one day. Not only that, but for the last two days the store has been unusually quiet, customer wise. I might be just over reacting but it just seems strange that's all."
"You have every right to be concerned. I'll ask around and see what I can find out."
"Thanks Mom. I can't afford to lose my business."
"Don't you worry my girl. I will personally make sure it doesn't come to that."

Adriana lay on her bed, sleep evading her. She sighed. What had possessed her to have sex with a man she hardly knew and on a public beach.? Her body gave a little quiver, as memories of their love making came flooding back. Even though on some unconscious level it felt wrong, she couldn't help taking pleasure in being wanted. The fact that she didn't really know him only seemed to heighten the excitement of it all.

# Chapter Ten

The next morning Adriana almost skipped into the kitchen. Her mother turned as she entered. "What's got you so cheerful this morning?"

The smile slipped from Adriana's face. "Nothing," she replied coolly, as she grabbed a coffee and headed back up to her room. Her mother smiled, knowing full well what was putting that extra bounce in her daughter's step. Adriana placed the coffee down on the dresser and threw herself onto the bed. Now that she had made the decision to see him it was all she could think about. Even when she had been with her husband, she hadn't felt the prickle of heat that shot through her whenever Hayden so much as looked at her. Could he be right? Would her husband have wanted her to be happy? Closing her eyes, she tried to visualise the last time she had made love with her husband. It had been wonderful and as always, she had felt fulfilled and loved. Her brow creased. There had never been that spark, no experimentation, no unchecked passion. He had always been soft and gentle, and so accommodating. The word boring sprung to mind and she quickly pushed it aside. She had never thought of their love making that way, not until now anyway. Her husband wouldn't have even considered doing what she had done only days before, on a public beach no less. Alistair had been the complete opposite to Hayden but she had loved him unconditionally and nothing would ever change that. Not even Hayden.

Adriana finished her coffee and began the mammoth task of deciding what to wear. After nearly an hour of trying on different items, she was finally ready. A smile played on her lips as she strapped on a pair of four inch heels which she knew would help accentuated the leanness of her calves. Drawing her hair across to one side she secured it in place with clips. She then applied a little mascara and eyeliner and ran some lip gloss over her lips. She wondered if she had just been another one of his many conquest? She sprayed a little perfume behind her ears and on her wrists. Giving a deep sigh, she took one last look in the mirror and turned towards the door. Quietly making her way down the stairs she slipped out of the front door unnoticed, managing to avoid her mother who was still busy in the kitchen. Her face broke into a smile, as she strolled out into the sunshine.

He kept looking across at the door. His behaviour had been inexcusable and he desperately needed to make amends. His body tensed when he saw her enter the cafe. He tried not to stare, but found it hard to draw his eyes away. As she made her way across the busy room her skirt danced invitingly around her slender thighs. His fists bunched as he remembered how her soft smooth skin felt under his touch. He felt himself harden and silently cursed under his breath. Taking a deep breath he forced himself to look away.

She spotted him the instant she stepped through the door. He was sitting at a table near the back of the cafe. A wooden screen partially obscuring him from view. Not wanting to appear too eager she let the smile slip from her lips. There was no way she was going to make a fool of herself yet again. As she neared the table, he glanced up. His eyes were icy cold. Her chest tightened. It was pretty obvious to her now, that he regretted their little liaison. She wished she had chosen something less flouncy to wear.

"Hi" she said trying to keep her voice level whilst giving him a strained smile.

He rose to his feet. "Thanks for coming" he replied, struggling to keep his emotions in check.

He walked around the table and drew her chair out for her. "Thank you," she said slipping into the seat, trying not to make eye contact and desperately hoping he hadn't noticed the pink tinge that had crept onto her cheeks. A warm tingle ran up her arm as his fingers brushed against skin. He snatched his hand away a little too quickly. Giving a little sigh, she settled herself in her seat. It was hard to imagine him feeling anything if he didn't want to. It was obvious she was setting herself up for a fall, if she kept expecting things that weren't there.

His body tensed as the soft scent of apricots drifted into his awareness. He glanced down at the soft pale flesh at the nape of her neck, wanting nothing more than to lay soft kisses upon her delicate skin. His fists clenched and unclenched as he made his way back to his side of the table and sat down. Snatching his beer up off the table he took a long hard swig. His eyes caught hers over the rim of the glass and he nearly choked. He placed his glass down on the table.

"Did you want something to drink? A wine maybe."

She shook her head. Her hands began to tremble she placed them in her lap where he couldn't see them. "So..., w...what was it you wanted to see me a...about" she asked hoping he hadn't noticed the slight quaver in her voice. He didn't answer. His attention was now focused on her glossy full lips. He fought the urge to lean over and taste them.

"Hayden."

Slowly he drew his eyes back to hers, giving her a glimpse of the warmth she knew existed. She smiled hesitantly. The warmth in his eyes instantly vanished. The feeling of rejection bit hard at her.

"I haven't got all day. I have a business to run. So what was it you wanted to see me about?"

His fist tightened under the table. What was it he wanted? Why had he even asked her here? In the back of his mind he could still hear the soft moans of pleasure that had escaped her lips as she had willingly responded to his touch. He gave her a smile that didn't quite reach his eyes. "I wanted to apologise for my behaviour the other day. It should never have happened."

She looked up at him, instantly drawing him in with her eyes. "There is no need to apologize."

He looked a little stunned, "But the other day on the beach, you...."

She gave a soft laugh, trying to make light of her predicament, "It was a spur of the moment thing, no strings attached, I get it," she replied, trying to cover the hurt biting at her.

He sat staring at her, not knowing what to say. Her reply had thrown him a little. The last time he had seen her she had been way beyond reasonable. He placed his hands up on the table. "I expected you to still be angry. I was all prepared for a lengthy apology."

Determined not to let him see how much all this was affecting her, she gave a little hesitant smile and reached over, placing her hands on his. It was hard not to react to the quick flare that shot through her.

"You're right, it should never have happened. But it did."

He withdrew his hand.

She drew herself up taller in her chair, "But to be completely honest, it was probably just what I needed."

He reached out and gently brushed his hand across her cheek. Heat instantly flooded her face, as she pulled away from his hand.

"Hayden please, don't do that," she blinked back her tears. Did the outcome of today really matter to her that  much? She looked across at him expectantly.

His jaw tensed, "I'm sorry."

She held up her hand. "Stop, please. I don't want to hear it." The last thing she needed right now was his rejection. The look on his face said it all.

"I don't understand. I thought that maybe you and I could..."

Her head shook slowly from side to side, "I don't do casual."

His jaw tensed, "Casual, who said  anything  about casual?"

"Come on Hayden, be honest, you're not looking for a relationship, you said so yourself. So I certainly wouldn't expect you'd be wanting one with a woman who has a three year old child."

He snatched the glass off the table  and emptied the contents in one gulp. Adriana nearly jumped out of her seat when he thumped the glass back down on the table.

"Why does everyone assume they know what I want?"

Her hands clasped in her lap, "You said you like the single life."

"I do. Well, to put it correctly, I did."

A crease formed on her brow, "I don't understand."

He leant forward and looked straight into her eyes.

"I won't let you walk out of my life." Her heart skipped a beat. "I've never  known  a  woman like you. I think about you constantly."

Scrapping the chair back, she shot to her feet. He reached out and captured her wrist before she could make her getaway.

"Hayden please... let me go. This isn't going to work. I have a daughter to think of. It's not just about you and me."

His grip tightened, "I've thought of little else for the last two days. I want to be with you, and your daughter. Please Adriana, just give me a chance."

Her eyes widened; was he actually pleading with her? Did she dare to believe what he was saying? Her eyes met his. This was the man who only days ago had ignited feelings in her which had been so powerful that she could think of little else.

"I don't know, Hayden." Her body gave a little quiver. His eyes darkened. "Adriana please, I know I have some flaws. I'm rude and arrogant, and at times downright mean, but I assure you, I do have some good qualities. Just give me a chance to show you."

Her lips twitched at the corners, "I think you can probably add honest as one of your better traits." Still she felt hesitant. "Firstly answer me this. Why would you want to commit yourself to a woman like me, who already has a child to another man? When you could probably have any woman you desired?"

"That's my problem right there. I desire you."

Adriana glanced up at him.

"For how long, until something better comes along?"

"I am not in the habit of using women. Oh I've heard the rumours; I promise you there is no truth to them."

I'm not sure if I'm willing to put it to the test."

"Trust me, I wouldn't lie to you. Why would I bother? As you said, there are plenty more women I could choose. But I want you."

"It's not just about me. I have a daughter to consider."

"When are you going to stop using your family as an excuse. You feel something for me I can see it in your eyes."

"Hayden. Please. It's not going to work."

"Says who, can't you at least give it a try." He took her hand in his. "Please Adriana, I can't stop thinking about you."

A smile touched her lips. "I suppose when you put it like that, how can I possibly refuse?"

His brow drew together, "So is that a yes?"

She smiled, "It's a tentative yes."

"We'll be good together, you wait and see."

"So where do we go from here?"

His eyes darkened, "We could start, where we left off."

Her cheeks flushed "Well, that I'm afraid is entirely up to you."

His brow creased, "Me, why?"

Adriana studied his face, trying to read his thoughts, "Am I to simply be just another notch on your belt or are you wanting more?"

His eyes narrowed, "That leaves me with very little choice."

Adriana's body tensed. "If you hadn't noticed I don't wear a belt."

She started to laugh.

"How about we agree to take this one day at a time, no pressure?"

Her heart leapt as he got up and walked around to her side of the table and drew her to her feet. He lowered his lips to hers and she instantly responded, melting against him, both now oblivious to the stares they were getting from some of the other tables. When he finally released her, her face was flushed and the colour of her lips heightened.

He grinned "How about we head back to my place?"

She gave a forced little smile, "I'm not sure I'm ready to be alone with you. Remember what happened last time."

He brushed his lips against her earlobe, "I'll be the perfect gentleman I promise?"

Her heart began to race at the thought of what they had already done on the beach. She nodded not trusting herself to speak.

"Good, because I can't stand not having you in my arms a minute longer." He nodded towards the door, "Why don't you head outside and wait for me while I go and pay for my beer."

She almost floated to the door. For the past few days all she had thought about was being with him again. There was no way she dared give herself time to analyse what she was about to do. A smile played on her lips; was her mother right after all, was a man in her life what she needed? It sure felt that way, she hadn't felt this happy in months, even years. She gave a sudden gasp when she was nearly knocked off her feet by a woman, as she barged in through the door. The woman gave loud impatient grunt.

"Why don't you watch where you're going?" she spat

viciously.

Adriana's eyes narrowed as she turned toward the woman "Excuse me! I think..."

The woman fixed her with a cold hard stare. "You! I should have guessed, rude as always."

Adriana stood staring, open mouthed. April's temperament certainly hadn't improved any. The hairs on the back of Adriana's neck bristled, but she was in a too good a mood to let it spoil her day. "No harm done," she said lightly.

April glared at her, "No harm done. I think at the very least you owe me an apology."

Adriana's eyes widened, "Me? If anyone needs to apologise it's you."

April gave an impatient huff, "Your sort shouldn't even be here."

Adriana's hands went to her hips, "My sort? And what exactly do you mean by that remark?"

April gave her a patronising smile "It's a bit expensive for the likes of you, isn't it?"

Adriana glared back "Excuse me, how dare you."

"Well... I've heard business isn't too good at the moment."

Adriana clenched her fists, aware that people were beginning to stare, "What did you just say?"

April smiled and went to move off.

Adriana felt like punching her square between the eyes. "How do you know about that?"

April stepped closer "I warned you not to mess with a Radcliff."

Adriana grabbed hold of her arm, "What have you done?"
April glanced down to where Adriana held her, "If you don't let go of my arm immediately, you'll have assault charges to add to your list of problems."

At that instant Hayden strode up "What the hell is going on here, Mother!"
Adriana released her grip and let her arm fall to her side. She stood looking from one to the other. Why hadn't she seen it before? They possessed those same cold grey eyes. The family resemblance was unmistakable.
Adriana turned to Hayden, "This is your mother?"
"I'm afraid so.... Why? What has she done this time?"
Adriana glared at him, "Why didn't you tell me you were a Radcliff?"
"It's not a big deal?"
Adriana gritted her teeth, "Obviously it is, otherwise you would have told me. You belong to one of the richest families in Maine. I on the other hand, work hard to earn enough money to pay the rent and put food on the table. Which, thanks to your mother is becoming harder and harder by the day."
His mother began to move away. Hayden stepped in front of her, blocking her way.
"What has she done?" Adriana looked up into his cold grey calculating eyes. "Why don't you ask her yourself." She hissed, spinning on her heel and hurrying up the street. Hayden looked back at his mother.
"You wait right here. I haven't finished with you yet."
He ran after Adriana.

"Adriana, wait please," he caught hold of her arm. "What the hell is going on? I thought we had everything sorted."

She spun to face him, "So did I. I don't appreciate being lied to. You deliberately withheld your identity from me. Why?"

"I don't know, I'm sorry, I was going to tell you."

"It's too late. If your mother is any indication of how you and your family operate, I'm not interested. Now kindly let me go."

He dropped his arm and watched helplessly as she stormed off up the street. His fists bunched as he strode back to the cafe. When he entered, his mother was already seated in one of the booths. He slid into the seat opposite her. "Mother, what was that all about?"

She smiled, "Shouldn't you be at work?"

"Stop trying to change the subject. I asked you a question."

Her eyes met his, "I'm not doing anything. If that woman doesn't know how to run her business, it's got nothing to do with me."

Hayden's eyes narrowed, "Mother I'm warning you. Stay away from her."

"Oh and why would that be? Don't tell me you have feelings for the poor woman."

"That's none of your business, Mother."

"Oh come now, surely you can't be serious. You can do better than the likes of her."

"Mother, I'm warning you. Stop before we both say something we will regret. Whatever it is you are doing to her, it will cease right this minute."

April grinned "Hayden, as the poor woman already pointed out, you are way out of her league. Forget her and move on."

He gritted his teeth "To a women of your choosing, no doubt."

"Of course darling. I know what's best for you. I always have.  Jessica is beautiful, intelligent and a very successful business woman. She is still more than willing to be your wife."

"Mother, you have manipulated people all your life to get what you want. What makes you think I would take any personal advice from you?  I won't bend to your rules; it is my life and you have no right to interfere in it."

She patted his hand, "I have every right. I'm your mother."

He gave an exasperated sigh, "Mother, I'm warning you stay the hell out of my life. It's none of your goddamn business."

She grinned, "Fine..., but don't say I didn't warn you."

He studied her, "What are you even doing here? You never come down to this side of town." His jaw tensed, "It was Jessica. She told you I was meeting Adriana here didn't she?"

"Come now Hayden. I know I meddle, but to even suggest such a thing, I think is preposterous."

Hayden looked doubtful, "Is it Mother? I don't think so."

He rose to his feet, "I'm warning you Mother. Stay away from her. If I find you've been interfering in her life in any way, there will be hell to pay."

His mother gave a patronising wave of her hand,

"Whatever you say, darling."

He shoved his hands into his pockets and strode out the door. How did his father manage to stay married to that woman for so many years?

April grinned as she watched his retreating back. It couldn't have worked out better. The woman would get all that she deserved. Now all she had to do was work out how to eliminate her from her son's life for good.


The intense look on his face was enough to have people stepping out of his path as he marched along the street, his hands still bunched into tight fists. He thought about going around to explain, but he was still too angry. It would be too easy to say the wrong thing and alienate her even more. He needed time to think. This had to be approached with caution. With that in mind, he decided the best option was to  head home. As he entered the house he kicked off his shoes and stripped off his shirt which he tossed onto the chair. He had been so close to having her in his arms again. If only his mother hadn't turned up when she did and ruined everything. He walked over to the drink cabinet and poured himself a stiff whisky. Opening the exterior door, he stepped out onto the veranda and made his way over to the rail. Even as he looked out over the bay he was reminded of her. He turned and threw the glass against the side of the house. It shattered on impact, spraying shards of glass across the surface of the deck. He watched as the brown liquid slowly ran down the side of the  house and dripped onto the deck.  It was about time his mother understood that she couldn't meddle in his life. At this rate he would end up old and alone, or even worse married to one of his mother's money hungry candidates. Maybe his mother was right. Would it be better if he simply walked away? Their worlds were so far apart, would she ever really fit into his? Would the pressure cause her to change? Wasn't it her independence and hidden passion which had attracted  him to her in the first place? Take those away and she'd be just like many of the other women he had met. He rubbed his temples, did he even need this right now?

# Chapter Eleven

Two weeks, three days and sixteen hours had passed since that fateful day at the cafe. At first she had wanted him to contact her, but as the days slowly slipped by, it became apparent that it wasn't going to happen. She steeled herself against the hurt, convincing herself that it was probably for the best. The silent phone only helped to confirm her decision. It was now plainly obvious what kind of man Hayden Radcliff was. If she never laid eyes on him or his mother again, it would be too soon. Her body gave a little shiver as she recalled the iciness in his mother's stare. That same frostiness had appeared in his eyes, not once but several times on the day he had rescued her. If she had only gone with her first instincts and walked away. There was no doubting that he could lay on the charm when the need arose, but he possessed an underlying nasty streak much like his mother's. If it hadn't been for April's interference she could have easily made the mistake of trusting him. Getting involved with a man like him wasn't a risk she was willing to take. There was no way that she would expose her daughter's happy trusting nature to either of them.

The bell on the store door tinkled, snapping her from her train of thought. Her breath caught in her throat when she glanced up and saw who it was. His facial expression gave little away as he strode across the store toward her. The door clicked closed behind him making the room suddenly feel smaller. She felt that she had prepared herself for a chance meeting. Now she realised when it came to him, there was no way for her to prepare. As much as she wanted to dislike him, he still had the ability to take her breath away. Her mouth went dry as he stood on the other side of the counter quietly assessing her. His eyes locked with hers. Adriana's face heated. The corner of his lips twitched upward. Her hands grabbed at the edge of the counter as she steadied herself.

"I... I," she ran her tongue over her dry lips. "I would appreciate it if you'd just turn around, and walk back out that door."

His eyes never left hers, "Is that what you truly want?"

She took a long swallow but couldn't bring herself to reply.

His eyes darkened, "I thought as much."

She dropped her eyes to the counter. "Hayden... please, just go."

"I'm not going anywhere until we discuss this. Look, I'm sorry... okay. I should have told you."

Her jaw tensed as she looked back up at him, "You think?"

His fists balled, "It's not as though we had a lot of time for talking."

Her flush deepened, "You seemed to have found plenty of time to find out about me."

"If I remember correctly, you offered the information. Look... I didn't come here to fight. It's not as though I deliberately set out to deceive you. I went about it the wrong way that's all, and I'm sorry. What more can I say?"

"I'm not asking for an apology. I can understand where you are coming from. That's why I think it's best we end this now before anyone gets hurt. I should never have let it happen in the first place."

He clenched his fists, "Don't say that. You and me..."

She looked away, "There is no 'you and me', can't you understand that? You're mother was right, we don't belong together. I would rather you forget it ever happened."

His eyes narrowed, "You can't mean that... How can you simply turn yourself off like that?"

"Things have changed; you are not who I thought you were."

"Why? Because I've got money, and a mother who's an interfering nasty old busy body?"

Adriana gasped at his directness.

"I didn't intentionally mislead you... Shit." He cursed

pushing his hand through his hair. "You need to understand why. I've had women..."

Adriana let out a groan, "I don't want to hear it."

He slammed his hands down on the counter, "Well, you're damn well going to, if you like it or not. They were pushed onto me by my mother and were only ever interested in my money.... With you, it was different... I was blind not to have seen it. Everything you say comes from your heart. That's what I like about you, there is no pretence."

"Unlike you."

"I deserved that."

Adriana sighed, "Look Hayden. Maybe I did misjudge you. But there is no way I'm going to subject Madison to the likes of your mother, or you for that matter."

"Me?"

She glanced down to where his hands were firmly gripping the counter. He followed her gaze. "I'm not like her." Adriana raised her eyebrows. "I've already warned her to stay away from you."

She looked back at him, "And you believe her?"

His eyes softened, "Actually no. But I'm working on it."

"You don't trust your own mother."

He stepped around the counter, causing her heart rate to accelerate.

"When it comes to my personal life, no. She's been trying to match me up for years. I've had to fend off, dodge, and at times be downright rude just to get them off my back and I'm not about to give up now."

Not trusting herself to be that close to him, she took a

step back. Her body came up against the edge of the counter. "Please Hayden... I can't, won't do this. I think it's better if we end this right now."

He moved closer placing his hands on either side of her, trapping her against the counter.

"Adriana. Look me straight in the eye and tell me you don't want to see me, and I will leave and never bother you again."

Her body went rigid; how could she possibly lie to him? She tried to steady her quivering limbs, "I, I don't want..."

He stepped closer, pinning her against the counter. "Don't want what?"

His eyes burned into hers, "I'm waiting. What's it going to be? Do I leave now, or are you willing to give us another chance?" He leant forward and brushed his lips across her throat. An almost inaudible little moan escaped her lips. He lifted her hair to one side, exposing the creamy skin of her neck.

Her eyes glistened, "You're not being fair."

He grinned, as he trailed soft kisses across her exposed skin. She drew  a sharp intake of breath as he nibbled lightly on her ear lobe. A small moan escaped her lips as he pressed himself against her, his muscular body now dominating hers.

"I'm still waiting," he whispered into her ear.

"O...kay., you... win."

His lips stilled. Adriana's eyes flared as she shoved against his chest, but he wasn't so easily moved.

"You might have  won, but I'm warning you. If your mother so much as  touches a hair on Madison's head....."

He smiled as he slowly began to guide her towards the back of the store. "That's what I admire about you. You are so passionate about the people you love."

"I'm warning you, if Madison doesn't like you you're history."

He grinned, "She'll like me, I can guarantee it."

"What are you doing? I'm working."

He glanced back at the empty store, "Looks like you have time for a break."

They entered the office. He kicked the door closed behind them. She bumped up against the desk. "Hayden, we can't, I..." His hands slid up under her shirt, his warm breath heated her skin. Her head dropped back and a small moan escaped her lips. His lips quirked as he brushed his thumbs against the underside of her breast. Her nipples peaked instantly.

"You're so beautiful" he murmured as he lowered his lips to hers.

She responded by nipping at his lip. His eyes darkened as he ground his pelvis against hers. A deep ache began to grow deep inside her. There was no fight left in her as she let him slowly undo the buttons on her shirt. He slipped it off her shoulders exposing her lace covered breasts. She fumbled with the buttons on his shirt and wrenched it open, her eyes hungrily devouring his body as she pushed the shirt down his arms. He pulled his hands free and let it drop to the floor. Wrapping his arms around her he surrounded her in his masculine scent. His male hardness pressed eagerly against her pelvis. He gave a low growl.

Her breathing quickened with every brush of his hand, her need grew stronger. His lips trailed across her skin. She felt completely engulfed by him as she stood pinned helplessly against the desk, her body now willingly surrendering to his.

The bell on the door sounded. Adriana froze. He had managed to make her forget where she was yet again. He gave a soft curse, as she pushed against his chest, "I have to...."

He held up his hand, "There is no need to explain. I should have realised. I wasn't thinking."

Adriana tried to ignore the throbbing between her legs. Never before had she felt so aware of her body's needs. She wanted nothing more than for him to take her right here on the desk. Her fingers fumbled with the buttons on her shirt. He gently slapped her hands away. "Here let me," he said, reluctantly doing up her buttons.

"Hurry up," she said impatiently.

He finished with the buttons and grabbed her around the waist before she could pull away, drawing her toward him. His eyes narrowed.

"We have to finish this," he growled.

She was fully aware of his hard body pressed firmly up against hers.

"Please, Hayden... I have to go."

"I'll let you go., on one condition."

Her eyes met his. "You have to promise to come out to my place tonight and finish this."

A small quiver ran up the length of her body.

"Hayden, I can't. My mother has had Madi all day. I can't expect her to watch her all night as well."

His grip tightened, "I'm not taking no for an answer."

"Hayden, please, I have to go."

"I'll make it easier for you. If you don't promise to come out to my place tonight I'll walk out of here right now, carrying my shirt over my shoulder and let whoever is out there?" He nodded towards the door, " come to their own conclusions as to what's been going on back here."

Her eyes narrowed, "You wouldn't."

He grinned, "Care to put it to the test?"

She had no doubt that he would carry out his threat.

"Okay, okay you win," she shoved against his chest with little avail.

"Not so fast. You have to promise."

"Hayden, please."

"Promise."

"Fine, I promise. Happy now?"

He released his grip.

She hurried to the door and opened it slightly to peer out. Mrs Bristol, the town busy body was already standing at the counter looking a little irritated. Adriana turned back to him.

"I promise okay..., now go please."

He pulled on his shirt and stepped up to her, lightly brushing his lips against hers. "Until tonight."

Quivering she gave him a forced smile, "Go."

He slipped out the back door unnoticed. Straightening her skirt, she hurriedly checked the buttons on her shirt then gave a quick glance in the mirror. Her cheeks were still a little flushed but there wasn't a lot she could do about that. Pasting on a smile she opened the door. Mrs Bristol gave her the once over and finding nothing amiss, began asking about one of the pieces Adriana had displayed in the window. For the rest of the day, Adriana found it hard to focus. Several times, customers had to repeat themselves just to get her attention.

# Chapter Twelve

Four hours later, she was standing in front of her mirror in her underwear, having tried on just about everything in her wardrobe. Defeated, she slumped down on the bed. What was she doing? She wasn't one of the childless sexy young women that she was sure he had had plenty of. A wife and a mother that was what she was. She gave a cynical little laugh, knowing she hadn't been anyone's wife for two years now. Hayden was the first man to break through her defences, and breakthrough he certainly had. Reaching up behind her neck she unclipped her locket and placed it in her jewellery box. If she was going to do this, then she was going to do as a single woman. The woman her husband had loved had long since disappeared. It was hard to accept that she now craved the company of another man. One she had only just met. A smile touched her lips as she picked up the new black stockings she had purchased on the way home. Opening the packet she pulled one out and carefully rolled it up her leg clipping it onto her new lace suspenders. She did the same on the other leg. As she rose to her feet she caught sight of herself in the mirror. The woman staring back at her was sexy and attractive. Seeing herself like that gave her the confidence boost she needed. Didn't she deserve to be loved? With renewed enthusiasm she finished dressing. Taking one last look in the mirror, she gave a satisfied smile, picking up her perfume bottle she sprayed a little on the underside of her wrists and behind her ears. She headed down stairs and made her way to the kitchen. Madison had already gone to bed. Her mother stood with her back to the door, doing the dishes. At the sound of Adriana's approach she turned. Her eyes widened and she let out a loud whistle. "You look sensational. This Hayden fellow is one very lucky man." Adriana began to feel a little uneasy, "You don't think it's a little too much?"

Her mother dried her hands and walked over to give her a hug. "You look beautiful, sweetheart. I feel like my long lost daughter is finally back."

Adriana placed a kiss on her cheek "thanks Mom."

Patricia motioned to the door, "Now go, have a good time."

Adriana walked up the hall, her mother following in her footsteps. When Adriana reached the door she hesitated. Patricia frowned and reached past her to open the door. "Adriana, if you back out now, I will personally throw you in the car and take you over there myself. Now go, I mean it."

Adriana smiled, "I think you actually do mean it. You're so bossy."

Her mother pushed her out of the door, "You had better believe it. I won't tell you again... go."

Adriana walked down to the car, unlocked it and slipped into the driver's seat. Turning the key she sat there for a minute, letting the motor run. A quick glanced back at the house confirmed that her mother was still watching from the doorway. Drawing in a deep breath, she slipped the car into gear and pulled away from the kerb.

A hard knot had formed in the pit of her stomach by the time she pulled her car into his driveway. After turning it off, she sat for a few minutes trying to convince herself that this was the right thing to do. Giving a deep sigh she got out and locked the car door. The nerves had began to take over as she approached the house. Light spilled out onto the front porch from the open doorway. A delighted gasp slipped between her lips when she spied the trail of rose petals leading into the house. A romantic; that was certainly a surprise, she thought as she followed the trail up the stairs through the front door and along the passage. He certainly hadn't seemed like the romantic type. She momentarily faltered when she suddenly realized she didn't know him at all. What was she doing? Her eyes followed the trail of petals that led out through the French doors onto the veranda. She moved to the door and peered out. As before it was empty. Her eyes widened. The garden was bathed in soft candle light. Hundreds of tea light candles, set in little rose shaped holders were lined along both sides of the path. The petals formed a trail leading down into the garden and along the path, before disappearing from view. She drew in a deep breath and followed them. They led her beyond the pond to the back of the garden. A small wrought iron table and two chairs had been placed on the paved area against the low rail fence which marked the boundary to his property. A freshly poured glass of champagne stood on the table. The bottle rested in an ice bucket next to it. Her brow creased, she was still alone. Taking the glass in her hand she took a long sip, hoping to steady her nerves. The smell of the sea drifted in on the breeze. She took a deep breath as her previous doubts begin to return.

He stood silently watching her. Earlier in the evening he had had his doubts about her keeping her promise. The extra effort he had made hadn't been in vain. His brow creased. A committed relationship was the last thing he had been looking for. Now here he was with a woman he was sure he could spend the rest of his life with. He smiled at her obvious discomfort. He liked the small insecurities that often showed through her otherwise capable exterior. His eyes travelled her body. Her black skirt hugged her rounded bottom. Glimpses of pale soft thigh showed through the long splits which ran from the hem of the skirt to the very top of her thigh. He had thought of little else but having her, since their little encounter at the store. As quietly as possible he made his way toward her. She let out a startled gasp when his arms slid around her waist. Her breath caught in her throat as he turned her to face him. The intense look in his eyes took another bite out of her already dwindling confidence. Her nipples hardened, wasn't this what she had wanted?

His eyes darkened. "Don't look so worried, I won't bite."

She glanced down at the glass, her hand was shaking. "I'm not."

He took the glass from her hand and placed it on the table. His raw sexuality began to overwhelm her. His hands slipped around hers. "I didn't think you would come."

"You went to a lot of trouble for someone you thought wouldn't turn up. I didn't take you for the romantic type."

"I thought you deserved it, after our first somewhat barbaric encounter."

She gave him a forced smile, "Barbaric has a certain appeal."

Her eyes drifted to his open shirt and his smooth toned chest beneath. A sudden wave of wanting washed over her.

His finger brushed along her cheek. "You look good enough to eat."

"You don't look half bad yourself."

Her long lashes fluttered across her beautiful green eyes. His gaze intensified.

She fidgeted under his scrutiny. Withdrawing her hands, she turned to look out over the bay.

"It's so beautiful here," she murmured softly, feeling a small tug of guilt as she looked out to sea.

He bought his body up against hers, wrapping his arms around her waist, sensing her slight hesitation, "You know how often I've dreamt of being here with you?"

She smiled, "You have?"

He laid  soft kisses up the side of her neck, "Every hour of every day since the first time I laid eyes on you."

"Surely you're not referring to the day you actually accused me of trying to drown myself?"

He grinned, "What can I say, one look into those beautiful green eyes of yours and I was well and truly hooked."

"Is that so? I'm not sure I believe you. For a man who obviously has a way with the ladies, you certainly took your time," she teased.

"Do you not remember our little encounter on the beach?"

"As if I could I forget. How you managed to convince me, I'm still not quite sure."

"You make me sound like some sort of predator and believe me you didn't need much convincing."

"You strike me as the sort of man who gets what he wants."

He laughed, "Possibly, but I have to admit you were rather easy prey."

She smiled, "I didn't put up much of a fight did I?"

He flipped her hair back off her shoulder letting his lips travelled down the length of her neck.

Her body began to relax, as his warm lips brushed against her cool skin.

She leant back against him, feeling his hard taut muscles press against her back.

"Champagne and rose petals; how is a girl to resist?"

His hands slipped up inside her shirt to cup her breasts. She let out a soft moan as his fingers found their way inside her lacy bra. He pinched her nipple gently between his fingers. With his other hand, he slowly released the buttons on her shirt. He slipped it off her shoulders and drew it down her arms, twisting it around her wrists trapping her hands behind her. His body pressed against her, making it impossible for her to get free. Her head dropped back onto his shoulder as his hands began to impatiently ravaged her body. He freed her breasts. A soft moan escaped her lips as his hands freely toyed with her nipples. She struggled against her bounds. The cool night air brushed across her heated skin, her body gave a little shiver. His weight shifted pinning her against the railing. She was now at his mercy. An urgent throbbing began to emanate from between her legs as he continued to toy with her. Never in her life had she ever felt so powerless. Before she knew what was happening he had unclipped her bra and pulled it and her shirt from her body, freeing her hands. He pushed her body forward pinning it against the railing with his body. A tortured groan escaped her lips as her sensitive nipples grazed across the rough weathered fence rail. He eased the zip on her skirt down. It slipped to the floor. He let out a deep groan.

"Jeezuss." He hissed between clenched teeth as his eyes took in the black silk stockings and lacy suspenders. Her tiny black G-string  giving her  minimal  coverage. The smooth pale skin on her buttocks glowed in the moonlight. Her hands gripped the rail as she heard him removing his clothing. She stared out across the moonlit bay. A sudden gasp escaped her  as her G–string was torn away leaving her fully exposed to him. Her body gave a little excited quiver, as the cool sea air brushed across her bare skin. He impatiently kicked away her clothing. Hooking his arm around her waist he drew the lower half of her body towards him. He eased her legs apart with his foot. His hand slipped between her legs as he sought out her moist centre, expertly drawing her to a quick and powerful climax. She cried out into night as he entered her with a powerful thrust. Her grip tightened on the railing as he drove himself into her, again and again. With every thrust of his pelvis, her nipples brushed across the rough timber railing. Again she felt her body began to climb, spiralling  slowly  upward.  She willing surrendered  to the powerful feelings now welling up inside her. Her body convulsed, sending her into a deeper more powerful release. He drove himself into her, gripping her hips tightly and giving her little choice but to accept what he had to give. A growl emanated from deep within his chest as he spiralled beyond control. His body tensed as he was  drawn to a quick and violent end.

He slumped against her, his breath coming in deep strained gasps. It hadn't gone exactly to plan. Guilt began to creep in. He had treated her no better than he had the first time. "I'm sorry," He whispered into her ear.

"I didn't mean for it to be like this. I just..."

"Don't! Don't you dare," she hissed.

"Here we go again," he thought to himself, as he stepped back releasing her from his grip, expecting a repeat performance of their last time on the beach. She spun around on him, her eyes sparkling, a wide smile creasing her face.

"Apologise..., don't you dare."

 His mouth dropped open. She leant back against the fence and grinned at him. Relief flooded through him as he stepped forward and pulled her into his arms, lowering his lips to hers. She responded willingly. Finally he found the strength to pull away.

"This is all your fault, you know."

Her eyebrows rose, "It is... and why would that be?"

His eyes moved to her stocking clad legs, "It was those black stockings and suspenders that did me in, you could have at least warned me."

"What, and spoil all the fun? Not likely." She shoved against his chest, sending him stumbling backwards. He fell awkwardly into the chair behind him. He glanced up at her standing there, her legs slightly parted. His eyes travelled from the black high  heeled shoes up the length of her stocking clad legs. Her pale skin glistened in the moonlight. She took a step closer. He reached out for her, but before he could get a grip she lifted one leg and pushed him back into the seat with her foot. She fluttered her eyelashes as she placed her foot on his lower abdomen. The long pointed heel of her shoes she strategically positioned just above his manhood. He froze, his eyes widened, "Careful."

Her eyes locked on his as she lowered the heel a little, so he could just feel the heel pressing against his scrotum.

She grinned, "So, how does it feel? Being at someone's mercy"

His brow creased then suddenly he smiled, "Kind of arousing actually."

Her eyes travelled the length of his body, "My point exactly. No apology needed."

When she placed her foot back on the ground he was quick to reach out and pull her down into his lap.

"How about we have a shower and you can pay me back? I'll let you do whatever you want, to me."

She considered it for a moment, "Deal" she leapt off his knee.

He gave her a dirty little grin.

Giving a little squeal she ran up the path, with Hayden in close pursuit. He snatched her off her feet and slung her across his shoulder slapping her on the bare backside. She giggled like a little schoolgirl.


Two hours later they lay on the bed completely exhausted. Adriana's leg was draped across his body. She lay there, watching the steady rise and fall of his chest as her mind mulled over the past few hours. A crease formed in her brow; was she silly to have put her heart at risk. for a man like him?

His eye opened, "Why the frown?" He rose up on one elbow and rolled her over on to her back.

Her hand instinctively moved to cover her stretch marks.

Hayden looked down at her hand "Please, don't do that."

"Do what?" she replied.

He gently pushed her hand away, "That."

"But they are so ugly."

He bent down and trailed soft kisses along each one of her scars. "They are part of you."

Tears sprung to her eyes, "I'm sorry."

He gave her a quizzical look, "For what?"

"For ever thinking you were like your mother. You're nothing like her."

He laughed, "You know, that's the nicest thing anyone's ever said to me."

"Hayden!"

He gazed down at her, wondering how he had managed to be so lucky.

"You've met her; are you telling me I'm wrong?"

Adriana blinked at him, "No..."

He lowered his lips to hers. At that precise moment she knew she had fallen in love with a man whom only weeks ago she wouldn't have given the time of day. Fate had thrown her a curve ball. If she hadn't been out at the beach that day, she may never have met him. Was it her husband who had inadvertently brought them together? She snuggled against him, ready to believe it was meant to be.

# Chapter Thirteen

Adriana woke with a smile on her lips. Everyday lately seemed like a good day. She quickly dressed and headed downstairs. Madison was sitting at the table eating her breakfast. Adriana kissed the top of her head, "Good morning sweetheart."

"Mommy, we have a clown coming to preschool today."

"Is that right? Won't that be fun? You'll have to tell mommy all about it when I get home." Adriana turned to her mother. "Mom, would be okay if I bought a friend home for supper tonight?"

Patricia's eyebrows rose. "Of course, you don't have to ask my permission."

"Whose coming Mommy?" asked Madison excitedly.

Adriana glanced at her mother then back to Madison. "Do

you remember the man you spoke to at the door, the day of your birthday?"

Madison's brow creased, "The man who made you cry."

"Yes, it wasn't him that made me cry. I told you he bought me back something that I thought I had lost."

Madison sat there looking at her blankly.

"He is a nice man."

"I won't like him."

"Madison, don't be so silly. You don't even know him."

"I don't want him here."

"Madison," Adriana snapped. "It is not for you to say who can and can't come to dinner. You are to be on your best behaviour. Do you hear me?"

Madison nodded. "I won't like him."

Adriana gave an exasperated sigh. Patricia slipped her arm around her shoulder.

"Don't worry yourself about it. I'm sure she will come around. You have to admit we haven't really had anyone to dinner for quite some time."

"I suppose not. I just want everything to go smoothly."

"It will Now stop worrying yourself over nothing."

They moved away from the table, "I'm not sure how he is with kids."

"Madison will come around, you wait and see."

"Hopefully pretty quickly. I'd hate it if they didn't get along. I've fallen for him in a big way."

Patricia smiled, "I promise you, everything will be fine. Now you get off to work. I'll have a little talk with Madison on the way to preschool".

The day ticked slowly by. The store was quiet which made the day drag. Hayden rang her in his lunch break to confirm their dinner date.

"Could you be there by six thirty?"

"Sure, would you like me to bring anything?"

"No, just your normal charming sexy self."

"I think I can manage that. I'll see you at six thirty sharp, then."

"Great... Hayden?"

"Yep."

"Umm, oh, don't worry, it was nothing. I'll see you at six thirty."

"I can't wait to see you."

"Me neither," she said, rather hesitantly.

"Is something the matter? You sound a little... unsure."

"I'm not, honestly... I'm just a little nervous, I suppose. I want you to like us, all of us."

"I know I will. Now stop worrying. I'll see you later."

The phone clicked down. She stood looking at the receiver. Was she being over dramatic? Surely he would be able to win Madison over, and her mother would probably be willing to settle for anyone as long as she was out there dating again.

After work she rushed home to get ready. She paced the floor as the clock slowly ticked around to half past. The doorbell rang. Nervously smoothing her hand over her hair, she went to open the door. He gave her one of his cheeky smiles and instantly all her doubts vanished.

"Hello, Gorgeous." He grabbed her and gave her a full deep kiss rendering her breathless.

She pushed against him, "Hayden, please."

He released her.

His eyes burned into hers, "Just be warned, I not leaving here without a goodnight kiss."

Her cheeks flushed under his intense stare. "You had better come in."

He stepped over the threshold. The smell of roast pork drifted up the hall.

"Mmm, something smells good."

"My mom's a great cook, I'm sorry to say I'm not half the cook she is."

His eyes darkened, "There are more important things than food."

Adriana glanced along the hall, "Shhh..., Mom might hear you."

He grinned, "I'm sure she would understand."

She slapped his chest, "You're incorrigible. Come and meet the rest of the family. I had better warn you though, Madison isn't so easily won over. She sees you as the man who  made me cry. I hope that's not going to be a problem?"

He flashed her a grin, "I'll use my witty charm."

"I think you might need more than that."

"We'll see."

They entered the kitchen together. Madison glanced up when they entered, eyeing him suspiciously.

Her mother wiped her hands on her apron and walked over to them. "Hayden, this is my mother Patricia. Mom this is Hayden."

Patricia smiled, "It's nice to finally meet you."

"Likewise, I can see where Adriana gets her beauty from."

Patricia had the same dark hair, as her daughter's, only sprinkled with a little grey. She was trim and fair skinned just like Adriana. Her eyes, however were more hazel than green. Surprising even him, she drew him into a full bodied hug.

"I've been dying to meet the man who has managed to put a smile back onto my daughter's face."

"Mom!"

"Well it's true." She released him from the hug. "You are more than welcome to pop around anytime you like."

Adriana gave her mother one of her looks. Patricia held up her hands.

"Fine, I won't say another word."

Adriana turned to see Madison staring at them. She took Hayden's arm and led him over to her. "Madison, this is Hayden, a very good friend of mine."

Madison sat silently, looking up at hm.

He crouched down beside her, "Hello there, Madison."

"Are you going to make my mommy cry?"

He smiled, "No, of course not.

"I don't like you."

"Madison, what did I tell you?" Adriana snapped.

Madison glanced up at her mother. Adriana shook her head.

"Madison, I promise you I would never upset your mommy."

"You promise?"

"Madison." Adriana snapped again.

Hayden turned and looked up to Adriana, "I promise."

Madison eyed him cautiously.

He smiled," What is that you are drawing?

She turned back to her drawing without answering. He pointed to a figure she had drawn.

"Who is this?"

"This is my Daddy and Rick and me and Mommy and this is our house."

"That is very good. Do you think you could draw me a picture?"

Her little face broke into a smile, "You can have this one."

He gave her a warm smile. "I would like that very much, but are you sure you want to give me this one?"

"I can draw lots if I want to."

"Thank you, Madison. I will hang it on my wall as soon as I get home."

Madison looked around at him, "Where is your house?"

"I live down by the beach."

Madison's eyes brightened. "I like the beach. Mommy showed me how to build sand castles."

"Is that right? Well maybe Mommy can bring you out to my house one day, and you can show me how to build a castle."

Madison glanced up at her mother. "Can we Mommy?"

"Sure you can, sweetheart. We will see what we can arrange.

Patricia walked over to them, "Why don't you all take a seat, and I'll call you when dinner is ready. Madison would you please clear your things off the table?" Without being asked a second time, Madison slipped from her chair and began collecting her crayons and paper.

"Would you like me to help you? Hayden asked.

Madison nodded shyly. He stood up and helped her collect her things, then followed her out of the room. He winked at Adriana as he passed. They walked up the hall and into her bedroom. Madison walked straight over to the desk by the window and lifted the lid. "The crayons go in here."

He obliged by dropping them into the desk. She left the picture on her bed.

"You can have it when you go home."

He smiled, "Okay. I like your room."

She smiled." I have a princess on my bed."

"I see that. Do you like princesses?"

She nodded, "I'm going to be a princess one day."

"Are you now? Well, I think you will make a wonderful princess."

"Mommy thinks I'm already a princess".

He smiled. "I think she might be right."

She began chatting to him about her dolls, and showing him her other pictures which were pinned around the walls of her room." What's this?" he asked, pointing to the yellow blob in the corner of one of the pictures. She gave a little sigh. "It's a puppy, silly."

"Oh, so it is."

He sat down on her bed as she went through her collection of soft toys, telling him the names for each one.

Adriana frowned as she glanced up the empty hallway. She rose to her feet and made her way towards Madison's room. Before she even got to the doorway, she could hear Madison talking nonstop. When she got to the doorway she gasped. Madison was leading him around the room by the hand showing him all her pictures. It was obvious she needn't have worried. Madison had already fallen under his spell. She should have guessed it wouldn't take him long to win her over. Her brow creased as she noticed nearly all the pictures included an image of Rick and Alistair. Would all the reminders of her past scattered around the house make him feel uncomfortable? If she had given it any thought she would have at least removed some of them; the house was littered with pictures of them. She shrugged. Well, it was a bit late now.

"If you two have finished, dinner is ready."

He turned and grinned at her, "Told you, you needn't have worried."

Her eyebrows rose, "I suppose I'll let you take credit where credit is due."

Madison turned and led him toward the door, "We had better go, Grandma doesn't like me being later for dinna."

Hayden shrugged as he was led past Adriana toward the kitchen.

"You can sit there," said Madison, taking the seat next to the one she had just offered him.

Adriana took the seat at the end of the table. He glanced over at her and smiled. Over his shoulder, she caught sight of the picture of her and Alistair. Their arms were

wrapped around each other and she was looking up at him adoringly. Suddenly she  felt as if her husband was watching her from every photo frame. Patricia noticed the change in Adriana's face as she walked over to place the food on the table. She followed her gaze,  noticing  the photo pinned to the fridge. Placing the food down on the table, she walked back over to the fridge and discreetly slipped it from behind the magnet and into her pocket. Adriana's eyes widened. Her mother simply smiled and went to get the rest of the food from the kitchen.
"Do you need a hand bringing anything through?" asked Hayden thoughtfully.
"No, this is the last of it, but thank you anyway."
Adriana met her mother's eyes. Patricia shrugged and placed the last plate on the table.

Several times throughout the meal, Adriana had to warn Madison to stop talking and eat her dinner. The atmosphere was relaxed and easy. She didn't feel nervous about him being here. He slotted into her family as if he had been sitting at their dinner table for years. After dinner he offered to do the washing up. Adriana dried as he washed. Patricia took Madison up to have a bath and get ready for bed.
"So, how do you think I measured up?"
"Don't go getting all smug on me. You know darn well she likes you."
"So all that worry was for nothing then?"
She flicked him with the end of the towel. "Ouch..., what did I do to deserve that?

"No...,' I told you so's'...alright?"

"Deal."

Adriana went quiet.

"Are you okay? If you're not comfortable with me being here you only have to say."

Her eyes moistened, "It's not that. I should have thought to remove some of his pictures. What with Madison drawing Alistair in every picture and giving you one. Every room in this household has at least three photos of him. "Doesn't it make you uncomfortable?"

"No why should it?"

"He was my husband, of course."

He turned and took Adriana's hands in his wet ones. "Look I understand, there is Madison to consider. The man died and lost his family for Christ sakes; what right do I have to get upset over a few photos? If anything, I should be grateful. If you were still married to him, I'm not sure I could cope."

"If I was still married to him, we wouldn't even be having this conversation. I would not have been out at the beach and therefore we would never have met."

He drew her into his arms "I know it sounds callous but I'm glad you aren't. Still married, that is."

Her eyes moistened, "Being with you is, different."

"Out of all the words in the dictionary you come up with 'different'. It's not much of a compliment."

"It wasn't meant to be. I'm still coming to terms with all the strong emotions you trigger in me. It was never like that with Alistair."

He drew her in and kissed her. Her cheeks flushed.

"See, that's exactly what I'm talking about. You shouldn't have done that..., not here. What if my mother or Madison had walked in?"

He grinned, "Would that be such a bad thing?"

"Yes, no, Oh, Hayden you make things so difficult."

His brow creased. "Do I, really?"

She glanced up at him, "No, it's me. I still need a little time. This has all happened so fast. I never imagined ever being with a man like you."

"I'm not quite sure how to take that."

"It's not a bad thing, I promise you. It just takes a little getting used to."

She smiled, "All I want is to get naked with you."

"Now that I can work with."

She placed her palm against his chest. But I have Madison to consider. She has spent most of her life being told about a father she never really got the chance to know. She likes you; that is a very good start, but please let me ease her into this slowly."

He kissed her lightly on the forehead, "I guess I can wait a little longer, on the understanding that we get to do a lot of that naked stuff you talked about."

"Hayden you could keep your voice down, Mom might hear you."

"I thought it was Madison we had to behave around, not your mother."

"Even so. I feel a little awkward discussing my sex life in this house."

"That's easily fixed." He drew her into another steamy kiss. "We won't talk about it, we'll just do it."

She slapped his chest. "Don't worry I'm just teasing. I'll behave I promise."

A little later after Hayden had been dragged along to Madison's room to read one bedtime story which turned into three, Patricia made her excuses and headed up to bed. Hayden listened for her footsteps as they retreated down the hall. Snatching Adriana's wrist he drew her onto his lap.

"I think that night went rather well, don't you?" His hand slipped up under her shirt."

"Please Hayden not here."

"You don't seem to be putting up much of a fight."

"I want this as much as you, can't you understand that? But I am in my mother's house and my daughter is asleep along the hall."

His eye's darkened, "I should go."

"Hayden, I didn't mean..."

He rose placing her on her feet. "I think it would be better if I went."

"I don't want you to go."

He grabbed her, drawing her against him, his taut muscles pressing against her.

"I can't stay here and not have you, can't you understand that?"

His hand moved down onto her buttocks, as he drew her pelvis against his. "I've behaved all night, now I'm alone with you..."

A little moan escaped her lips. "I have trouble resisting you."

"And I, you," he growled pushing her away. "Which is why I have to go."
Reluctantly she saw him to the door. Two more near fatal kissed took place on the door step.
He grinned, "I hope none of the neighbours are watching."
She glanced along the darkened street, "I think we are fairly safe."
His hand glided up her bare thigh. "I could take you right here right now."
Her body quivered. "You were supposed to say, No."
"I'm not sure I can."
"Jeezus, Adriana, you aren't making this any easier."
She pulled her skirt back down, "You had better go."
He leant over to kiss her.
"No I can't..., please just go. I'll see you tomorrow."

She watched him walk down the path. It would be so easy to call him back and take him upstairs. But could she risk Madison catching them? She gave a heavy sigh. There would be time to make it up to him. Once she had explained their situation to Madison. He gave her a wave as he slipped in behind the wheel. He took one last look before driving off down the street. There was no way he was going to manage to get to sleep tonight. He looked forward to a time when he would be able to stay the night.

# Chapter Fourteen

Adriana looked up and smiled as the door opened and Hayden strode in.

"Hello gorgeous." He kissed her softly on the lips. "Are you ready?"

"For you, always."

He had been calling in everyday to take her to lunch. It was wonderful to again have a man lavish his affection on her. He was always the gentleman and insisted on paying for everything. She didn't mind, but she had drawn the line at him helping her out financially. That, she felt was crossing the line. Locking the store door she slipped her arm through his.

"So where is it to be today?"

"We're taking the cheap option today. I thought maybe a picnic in the park."

Her head dropped against his shoulder, "Sounds divine."

That was the things he liked the most about her. She never expected anything, and had even put a cap on what he was allowed to spend on her. It was a little frustrating for him at first, but now that he knew her better, he understood. Their lunches were the only thing she hadn't put restrictions on. He kissed her forehead; the fact that she didn't care about his money was a welcome change to the money hungry women he had met in the past. The truth was that she was a very passionate woman whom he couldn't seem to get enough of. He smiled down at her. Her eyes turned up to his.

"What's the silly grin for?"

A mischievous glint appeared in his eye, "I was thinking about last night."

She blushed. He laughed, "You come across so innocent. If people only knew what you were capable of."

Her hand slapped his chest. "Hayden, stop it."

"I can't help it, you drive me wild."

She smiled, "the feeling's mutual." Who would have thought that she, of all people would be in a relationship with one the most eligible bachelors in town?

Ross watched them make their way down the street. His body stiffened as he saw Hayden lean in and kiss her on the lips. His anger rose. He had always hoped that he and Adriana would someday be together. He hadn't meant to fall in love with her. It was obvious to him now that she would never feel the same way. He stomped back into the store, slamming the door behind him. What did she see in a man like that? He had a reputation for being a callous womanizer. She would only end up being hurt. It had been weeks now since she had been over to see him. Instead she chose to spend her time with him. Hadn't she promised to tell him when she was ready to date. Obviously it had slipped her mind. Now she was risking her reputation by being seen with a man who had a shocking reputation. Why would she even consider lowering herself to that level? What future could they possibly have together? He had to find a way to warn her, before it was too late.

Hayden led her towards a quiet corner of the park, under the shade of a large tree. A blanket had already been spread across the grass. He sat down resting his back against the tree and pulled her down beside him. Stretching his long limbs out in front of him, he gave a contented sigh, "This is the life."
Adriana snuggled up against him. She was so blissfully happy that she hadn't even given poor Ross a second thought. Hayden opened the picnic basket and pulled out what appeared to be a very expensive bottle of wine. He lifted out a small container, and handed it to her. "I think this one is yours." It was a rather large serving of boysenberry cheese cake.
"You've gone to so much trouble."
He smiled "Not me exactly. I had the receptionist come down here and set it all up."
"Even so, I appreciate the effort you've gone to."

He brushed a stray lock of hair from her face, "Anything for my girl."
She gave a long sigh; summer would soon be over and picnics in the park would no longer be possible. Her business always quietened down over the winter months. Things hadn't been going so well lately. Sales were well down on last year. If things didn't pick up soon she may have to consider closing the store and getting herself a job.

Hayden's eyes travelled the length of her body, "There's a carnival down on the pier on Saturday." Adriana looked up at him. "I would like to take you and Madi, if you're up for it."
She smiled, "That would be wonderful. Madison would absolutely love it."
"If you want, we could shoot down the coast a way's and make a weekend of it."
She hesitated, "What about the store?"
His brow creased. Her hand waved in the air, "It's been quiet anyway. One weekend won't make any difference."
"Good, then I'll make the arrangements."
Adriana turned to him, "It would have to be separate beds."
He pulled a roll out of the basket and handed it to her "You still don't want Madison to know that we're sleeping together? Can I at least ask why?" He waited for her to empty her mouth, as he pulled out a roll for himself and began eating.
"I don't know..., it just doesn't feel right. Not yet,

anyway."

"Adriana we have been going out for over a month now. Don't you think it's about time you let your daughter know? Why the hesitation?" He took her hand, "Are you still worried I'm going to tire of you? I promise you I'm not going anywhere."

Her eyes pleaded with him, "Hayden, please don't make this more of an issue than it is. I just need a little more time, that's all."

He gave an exasperated sigh, "Fine. If it's really that much of an issue. You and Madi can share the double bed and I'll take the single one. But be warned I'm not going to stay as your good friend forever. You are going to have to tell her.., the sooner the better."

She smiled, "you'd do that for me? Take the single bed?"

"Begrudgingly."

"Thank you," she placed a kiss on his cheek.

He grinned, "Don't thank me yet, you still have to fend me off. Now eat, I have to get back to work and sort out a few things before we go."

An hour passed before he reluctantly got to his feet. He reached down and pulled her up. Dragging her against him he kissed her passionately on the lips. His hands slid down over her backside as he drew her close pressing his pelvis against hers. Adriana flushed, as she caught a passing man's eye.

"Hayden..., people are watching."

"Let them," he growled softly in her ear. He released

her.

"So what time does this thing start on Saturday?" she asked.

"This 'thing' as you so eloquently put it, is called a carnival and it starts around nine in the morning. I was thinking maybe if I picked you both up about ten."

"Sounds perfect, is there anything you want me to bring?"

"No, everything's sorted. Just what you need for yourself and Madison. Pack light, you won't be wearing much."

"Hayden! He grinned "Don't worry I'll try to behave myself..., when Madison's around."

She eyed him suspiciously, "I'm not sure I can trust you. Do you even know how to behave?"

He gave her a sly grin, "Oh Ye of little faith."

"Fine. I'll trust you to be discreet, how's that?"

"I think I can work with that." After giving her another lingering kiss, he reached down and picked up the picnic basket and blanket. "By the way, be sure to pack a nice skimpy bikini."

She tensed, "I don't swim."

He smiled, "We'll see."

"I'm not joking Hayden. I won't go into the water."

His brow creased, "Bring that bikini anyway,' he raised and lowered his eyebrows in quick succession. "It wasn't swimming I had in mind."

"You said you would behave." She said, giving him a sharp poke in the chest.

He grinned, "I think the word was discreet. There is a difference."

She laughed, "Go, before I change my mind."

He turned to leave, "Is there any way you can get away tonight?"

"No sorry, Moms going out."

His disappointment was obvious, "I could pay you a late night visit."

She shook her head, "Lunch tomorrow, that's my best offer, take it or leave it."

"Tomorrow it is." He gave her a quick kiss on the cheek and headed across the park. It was hard not to take him up on his offer of a late night visit. It wouldn't be right though, not in the same bed she and her husband had shared.

Saturday rolled around pretty quickly. By nine o'clock Madison was already driving Adriana mad, asking every five minutes when Hayden was going to get there. Adriana  breathed a sigh of relief when she finally heard the truck horn sound outside. Madison threw open the front door and rushed down the front steps. She bounced up and down on the curb, her excitement bubbling over. Hayden slid out from behind the wheel and walked around to where Madison was waiting. Madison beamed up at him then leapt into his arms. He lifted her up in the air and swung her around in a big circle as she squealed with delight. He tucked her under his arm. She giggled, as he walked towards the house.

"Hmmm, I wonder where Madi is? Madi" he called. "Where could she be? I told her to be ready when I got here. Maybe she doesn't want to come anymore?"

Madison let out  a loud squeal and wiggled frantically in

his grasp.

"I'm here" she cried.

He stood her on her feet.

'Oh, there you are. Are you ready, like you promised?"

"Yep," she replied nodding. "Mommy packed my bucket and spade."

Hayden smiled, as reality hit. He loved this little freckle faced girl as if she were his own. She looked up at him, her green eyes dancing with excitement, "Are we going to a car..., cani, cann..."

Hayden crouched down in front of her "Carnival," he said smiling.

She grinned, clapping her hands together, "yes, carn...ial.

He laughed. "Where is your Mommy?"

Madison glanced back at the door.

"Mommy's coming now. She's grumpy."

When Adriana didn't appear, Madison took it upon herself to run in and get her. Hayden could hear her running through the house calling out for her mother. He smiled when she returned with a very harassed looking Adriana in tow. The frown dropped from her face the instant she saw him.

"I could do with a hand" she said, dropping one of the bags she was carrying.

Hayden strode the length of the path and scaled the steps before she had a chance to juggle what she was holding, so she could reach down and retrieve it. He snatched it up and gave her one of his heart stopping smiles, "At your service madam."

She gave him a seductive little smile, "Now..., that would

be nice."

His eyebrows shot up, "I thought we had to behave this weekend."

"I said you had to. I didn't say anything about me."

His eyes widened, "And how's that fair?"

She pushed past him, "Who said anything about being fair?"

He followed her out to the truck. It was going to be hard enough to restrain himself without her teasing.

Once they had packed the car and had Madison strapped safely in the back seat they headed off. Madison chatted constantly, asking one question after another, wanting to know everything there was to know about carnivals. By the time they arrived down at the pier and found a park, both Adriana and Hayden were glad to get out of the car. Adriana saw to Madison while Hayden went to pay for the parking. By the time he returned Adriana and Madison were already standing beside the truck waiting for him. He smiled at the sight of them. Was this what it was like to have a family? He had never thought of himself as a family man. Suddenly he realized how much he wanted it and a smile formed on his lips. "What are you grinning about?" Adriana asked as he approached them. His hand slipped into hers, "I was just thinking how lucky I was to have the both of you in my life."

Her eyes turned up to his, "I know just what you mean." Madison had already had a glimpse of the carnival and was now impatient to get moving.

"It's a bit of a walk back to the pier. I hope Madison doesn't get too tired."

Hayden smiled, "I think I can fix that," he took hold of Madison around her waist and swung her up onto his broad shoulders. Madison squealed with delight. Slipping his hand back into Adriana's, they headed off towards the carnival.

Madison got more excited the closer they got. From her high vantage point she could already see some of the happenings behind the fence. Now impatient to join in the fun, she fidgeted constantly. Hayden lifted her off his shoulders as they approached the gate. He took her by the hand and crouched down in front of her, "Madison, look at me." Reluctantly her eyes turned to him. "We can't have you running off. There are a lot of people here. You could get lost." Her attention drifted back to the carnival. "Madison, are you listening to me?" She turned back to him and nodded. "If you behave yourself and do as I ask, you get to ride on any of the kiddie rides you want. But you must stay with us at all times, is that understood?"

Madison nodded her head. As he stood back up she placed her little plump hand in his. Hand in hand they walked toward the ticket booth. A lump formed in Adriana's throat as she followed behind them. She blinked back tears. Madison had already missed out on so much. Hayden turned at that moment, as if reading her thoughts. He reached for her hand. Together they entered the carnival grounds. Hayden was true to his word, as

Madison was placed on ride after ride.

Adriana couldn't help but smile. He looked a little out of place with  his long legs draped over a carousel horse. Madison waved frantically. He clutched at her securing her in place in front of him, as she let go both hands from around the bar. Hayden appeared to be enjoying it as much as Madison was. Madison was still laughing when the ride finished and  Hayden lifted her off.

"How about we all go and get an ice cream?"

Madison clapped her hands, "Can I have a pink one?"

"Madison, where are your manners?" Adriana scolded.

Madison head tilted to the side as she looked pleadingly up at Hayden, "Pleeeese?"

Hayden laughed, "A pink one it is." Madison slipped her hand into his.

"Right this way, little miss." He held out his other arm for Adriana. She sidled up to him as he draped his arm around her shoulder. Yes, he thought, his very own little family. They sat down in the shade and ate their ice creams. After they had finished, Madison lay her head down on her mother's lap and drifted off to sleep. Hayden stared down at her. Madison was certainly going to be a beauty just like her mother. Adriana glanced up, "What now?"

"I think we had better head back to the truck."  He stood up, scooping Madison into his arms. Madison gave a little murmur and snuggled against him.

Adriana linked  her arm through his as they

strolled back along the pier. They passed a row of stalls selling handcrafts. She glanced over. As if reading her mind Hayden steered them over toward the stalls. Adriana glanced up at him, "She's not to heavy is she? I could always leave it for another time."

"Take your time, have a look around." He shifted Madison in his arms, as Adriana slowly made her way through the stalls, talking to the various artists and leaving her business card. As she turned the corner into the next row of stalls she came face to face with Leslie.

"Oh, hi" said Leslie, finding it hard to look Adriana in the eye.

Adriana smiled, "How are you?"

"I'm fine" she replied, looking even more uncomfortable.

"So when did you get back?"

Leslie looked away, "Oh, um.., last week."

"You should come by the store. We could put your crafts back on display."

Leslie fidgeted, "Umm..., maybe I will."

Hayden strode up beside them and smiled. Leslie's mouth dropped open, as she looked from Adriana to Hayden, then to the sleeping Madison nestled contently in his arms.

"Oh, Leslie this is Hayden. Hayden, this is Leslie. A former client of mine."

"Nice to meet you," he replied, giving Leslie one of his famously charming smiles.

Leslie stood there open mouthed, unable to speak. Hayden turned to Adriana.

"I'm just going over there under the shade, to wait for you. It's getting a bit hot out in the sun for Madi."

"Oh right. I'll be there in a minute."

He smiled, "No rush," he turned to Leslie. "It was nice to meet you, Leslie."

Leslie simply nodded. They both watched him stride away. Leslie took hold of Adriana's arm, "You're seeing him?"

Adriana smiled, "Yes..., I am."

Leslie's brow creased, "Why?"

Adriana looked across at Hayden, now sitting on the grass under the tree. Madison was still sleeping against his chest. When she turned back she saw that Leslie's eyes were wide with horror.

"What's the matter?  You have gone awfully pale."

"Oh Adriana, you have no idea have you?"

Adriana's brow creased. "I don't understand."

 Leslie gripped her arm tightly." He's the reason I pulled out of our contract. He threatened to fire  Sam if I didn't. My Sam works at the Radcliff's paper mill."

Adriana's body stiffened, "That can't be," she glanced back over at Hayden, "He wouldn't."

Leslie's eyes narrowed, "Well he did, and I heard the same happened to two more of your clients. There has also been a bit of gossip going around town, about your products not being genuine. They are saying you bought them in from overseas."

Adriana face paled, "Who's been saying such things?"

"It's not true, is it?"

"Of course it's not. Why would I bother to get local artists like you if it  was?" She glanced over at Hayden.  Was his interest in her purely to put her out of business?

"I'm going to put a stop to this right now."

"Adriana wait... I'm not..."

Adriana spun on her heel and stormed over to where Hayden sat under the tree with Madison cradled in his arms.  Her eyes glistened, how could he do such a thing? She stood glaring down at him, "I would like to go home..., now!"

He looked up at her bewildered, "why? What's happened?" Her hands went to her hips.

"You could say that I've been enlightened about a few things. I should have realised a leopard doesn't change his spots."

He rose to his feet, Madison shifting  in his arms. His brow creased. "Are you angry with me?"

She gave a loud humph, "Very perceptive of you."

He rolled his eyes, "So are you going to tell me what it is that I am supposed to have done?"

"I think you already know. How could you do such a thing? Give Madison to me," she said, reaching for her. "We'll find our own way home."

He pulled Madison away, "I not doing anything of the sort until you tell me what the hell is going on here."

"It's to do with you putting me out of business. I suppose now you are going to deny it."

"What! That's ludicrous. Where an earth did you get such a stupid notion."

"Oh so I'm stupid now, am I? Well let me tell you, the only stupid thing I did, was trusting you. Now give me my daughter."

Madison stirred in his arms.

"Adriana calm down. Can't we talk about this like civilised adults?"

She made another reach for Madison; he snatched her away.

"Adriana, if you could just hear yourself."

"People like you are all the same, you think you can just run over the little people. Well, I'm telling you now. This one is not going down without a fight."

"Are you for real? I have done nothing but be here for you. Now you're accusing me of god knows what. Where did you hear all this garbage?"

Her shoulders slumped, "Leslie said you threatened to fire her husband, if she didn't remove her things from my store."

His jaw dropped open, "What! Me...?" He glanced across at Leslie's stall, but couldn't see her. "Leslie told you this?"

She nodded. "She most certainly did."

"And you believed her."

She fixed her eyes on him, " Why wouldn't I. What reason would she have for lying?"

Her eyes moistened, " So it wasn't you?"

"Of course it damn well wasn't. What do you take me for? What would I have to gain?"

She hesitated, He was right. A lump caught in her throat. Her eyes dropped to the ground, "Then it must have been your mother."

His body tensed, "Now you're just grasping at straws. My mother may be many things, but I don't think even she would stoop that low."

Adriana glanced up at him, "I think she would."

"Why?"

"Because I upset her, that's why. She threatened me. I never thought she would carry it out. That day at the cafe, she knew my business was having difficulties. How could she have known that?"

His eyes met hers "Adriana, I'm hoping you are wrong, but now that you mention it, there are a few things that don't add up. You should have told me things weren't going well."

"Why, so you could ride in on your white horse and rescue me? No thanks, I've come this far on my own and I don't need rescuing."

"I suppose I should have seen it coming." His eyes sought hers, "I promise I'll fix this."

She gave him a forced smile, "I should be the one apologising. I should have known you wouldn't have had anything to do with it... I was angry and wasn't thinking straight. I'm so sorry."

"I'm still a little hurt that you thought I had something to do with this."

She looked up at him, "I'm sorry, Hayden. I really didn't mean to say those things, but you said you were going to put a stop to your mother's antics."

He tensed, "I couldn't very well fix something I knew nothing about, could I?  You never even hinted that your business was in trouble."

"As I said, I didn't want you thinking you had to jump in and rescue me."

He placed his arm over her shoulder and drew her close,

"When it comes to my mother, it's not rescuing it's protecting. I'll go and talk to Leslie and see if I can't sort this out."

Adriana nodded, "Be gentle with her, she didn't mean any harm."

Madison stirred as he handed her over to her mother. His shoulders felt tense as he walked over to the stall. What had possessed her to think it was him? He had been nothing but kind and supportive to both of them.

It seemed forever before she saw him coming back towards them. His mouth was set in a firm line. The tension in his body was obvious, "I should have known my mother was behind this. I assured Leslie that I had nothing to do with it, and my mother doesn't hold the power to fire anybody; not without the Board's support. I apologised for all the grief my mother has caused her family and assured her that her husband's job is perfectly safe; along with any others which have been threatened." He shook his head. "I have worked alongside all these men, and it infuriates me that my mother thinks she can meddle in people's lives."

Adrian reached up and kissed him on the cheek, "I should never have doubted you. I'm so sorry."

"Leslie will be in on Monday morning to renew her contract. She's is going to contact the others and suggest they do the same," he said gruffly.

Adriana glanced down at the sleeping child in her arms. "You're too good to me."

His eyes softened, "That's not entirely true." Her body

tensed.

"I've let my mother have a free rein, for far too long. All this could have been avoided if I had been paying a little more attention."

"You can't be expected to keep tabs on her, twenty four hours a day."

"I suppose not, but even so I feel partly responsible. She could have put you out of business."

"I don't think it would have come to that," she replied, feeling the need to lie.

"I'll tell you one thing. My mother has a big wakeup call coming next week." He brushed his hand along her cheek, "You do know that I would never do anything to harm you, right?"

Her eyes moistened as she nodded her head. Madison weight was putting her arm to  sleep, so  she  shifted  her onto the other shoulder.

"Here, give her to me."

She willingly passed Madison across to him. Madison blinked her eyes sleepily,  then closed them again.

"I think she is well and truly worn out."

Adriana slipped her arm through his, "Maybe it's time we headed back to the truck."

"It would be a good idea to get started. We have a fair way to go."

Adriana glanced up at him, "You still haven't said where we are going."

He grinned, "And I'm not going to."

She squeezed his arm, "I will make it up to you. I should never have doubted you."

He raised his eyebrows, "Sounds promising."

Her eyes met his, "I will never doubt you again, I promise."

"I'm glad to hear it, now let's get out of here."

# Chapter Fifteen

It took them an hour and a half to travel down the coast. Madison thankfully slept the whole way. They pulled up outside a rather expensive looking hotel. Adriana was tempted to say something about the extravagance, but quickly thought better of it, thinking she had probably given him enough grief for one day. Madison woke up the instant the car stopped and rubbed her face irritably. Adriana and Hayden glanced at each other and smiled. They got out and started unpacking the car. By the time they were settled in the room, Madison was back to her usual bubbly self.

They ate an early dinner, then headed off down to the beach. The moment they hit the sand Madison ran off to try out her new bucket and spade. Hayden spread out a blanket and  sat down,  patting the ground beside him. Adriana gave a quick glance down the beach. Madison was happily playing in the  sand, so she sat down beside him.

"If someone had told me three months ago that I would be sitting here on a beach with you, I would never had believed them."

He smiled, "Honestly,  I wouldn't have believed it either." The sky began to turn a beautiful shade of pink as the sun slowly crept towards the horizon. Adriana snuggled up against him. Their focus was drawn toward Madison playing further down the beach in the sand. He gave her a gentle squeeze.

"This was something I always wanted as a child."

Silence settled between them. "I never had this growing up. I don't remember ever going out as a family, unless it was to a lunch with some business associate of Father's. We would all be dressed up in our best clothes, and have to sit quietly for hours bored out of our little minds."

Her hand moved to his chest as she reached up and kissed his cheek. "Well, you have it now."

He smiled, "I have, haven't I? You know, I swore I wasn't going to be like my father, god rest his soul. He was driven by his greed for money and power. Sometimes I wish I could just walk away, and leave it all behind and everything it stands for."

She glanced up at him, "I never knew him but I guessing you're nothing like him."

His brow creased, "Maybe I was more like him than I chose to  admit. You showed  me there is more to life and that life doesn't always go to plan."

"If you left Radcliff's, what would you do?"

He shrugged, "Who knows? Don't get me wrong. I enjoy working with the men in the mill. I wanted to show them that not all bosses are like my father was. Some of us actually care."

She brushed her hand across his chest, "You have a kind heart, you know that?"

"Hmm., maybe, but don't go telling everyone. I think there might be some women in town who would contest that."

She smiled, "We'll call that self defence."

He laughed, 'That's a new one."

She lay her head on his chest, "You know, there is no other place I'd rather be, than sitting here with you."

He kissed the top of her head, "I never thought I'd say it, but I feel the same. My life such as it was, revolved around the mill. I may not have been as focused on money as my father, but I still spent a majority of my time there. Life was actually passing me by and I didn't even realise it."

"Well now you can make up for lost time. Have you ever built a sand castle?"

His brows drew together, "No, I can't say I have."

She pushed away from him and leapt to her feet. Taking his hand she tried to draw him up. He resisted. "Come on. We can't have you going through life without experiencing the thrill of sand castle building."

He reluctantly got to his feet, "Lead the way, but be warned I have no skills in this particular field."

She laughed as she dragged him down to where the receding tide had dampened the sand. Dropping down onto her knees she began digging in the sand with her hands. He stood watching, unsure of what to do. Her eyes shone with excitement when she turned to look up at him.

"Well., are you going to help or not?"

"Not, I think."

"Come on, it won't hurt a bit, I promise."

He dropped to his knees beside her and followed her lead. "Can you at least give me some idea of what I am supposed to be doing?"

She grinned, "That's the beauty of it. We make it up as we go along."

Madison rushed over to join in. They worked side by side; their hands would touch and they would glance up at each other and laugh.

When they were nearly finished Madison used her new bucket to carry bucketfuls of water in hope of filling the moat they had dug around the base of the castle. After the fourth trip, she threw down the bucket in frustration. Hayden dug a small trench out to the water, and they watched as the waves washed in and filled the moat. Madison found great delight in finding shells for the windows and a stick for a flagpole. Finally a piece of driftwood was placed down for the drawbridge. He smiled, as he watched them putting on the last shell, knowing there was no place he'd rather be.

By the time they had finished, it was almost dark.

They stood back and studied their masterpiece in the moonlight.

Hayden glanced over at her, and began to laugh.

Adriana looked over at him.

"What?"

"Your face is covered in sand."

She brushed the back of her hand across her cheek and made it even worse. He reached over to assist, then realised that his hands were also covered in sand. She laughed. It was such a wonderful sound. He couldn't remember ever hearing his parents laugh. Seeing her standing there, looking at him with those beautiful, big innocent green eyes reminded him of the day he had first met her. Who would have thought that a chance meeting on a lonely stretch of beach would completely change his life?  He took her sand covered hand in his and pulled her against him, kissing her softly on the tip of her nose, the only part of her which didn't appear to be covered in sand. She leaned against him, feeling the warmth of his body through his thin shirt. Madison gave a little giggle. They both turned to find her staring up at them. Hayden bent down and lifted her up into his arms.

"And what's so funny?"

"You kissed Mommy's nose."

He leaned forward and lightly kissed hers. She giggled, screwing up her little button nose then reached up and kissed the end of his nose,  setting them all off into fits of laughter.

Adriana and Hayden walked up the beach hand

in hand, Madison was up on Hayden's shoulders, her bucket clutched in her little hand, depositing loose sand all over his shirt. Madison gave a little yawn.

"I think it might be someone's bedtime."

Madison blinked her eyes slowly, now too tired to protest. Adriana grinned up at him.

"She'll sleep like a log tonight. We could put her in the single room."

He instantly caught her meaning and pulled her against him. Anybody watching would think they looked like the perfect little family.

When they got back to the hotel room, Madison was bathed and put to bed. Adriana pulled her door closed and glanced up at him, not needing to say a word. She brushed past him and walked into the bathroom to run a bath. He followed behind her, an all too familiar glint appearing in his eyes.

A smile touched her lips. "If you promise to behave yourself, I might be willing to share my bath."

His eyebrows rose, "I thought that was off limits this weekend?"

Her eyes sought his, "I might be persuaded to change my mind."

Turning off the taps, she began to undress, "Anyway, I said you couldn't share my bed. I didn't say anything about my bath."

She stepped into the bath and sunk down into the water. He started to strip out of his clothes. The weekend had suddenly become a whole lot more interesting. A smile touched her lips as her eyes roamed his naked body.

"Care for some company?"

Scooting down the bath, she made room behind her. At times, she still found herself wondering what a man like him saw in her. The day she had met him, she had thought him cold, heartless and downright rude. If anything, he was exactly the opposite. He had a soft heart; not that he would admit it. She knew a side of him that very few people knew. He slipped in behind her, stretching his long muscular legs down either side of her body. He rested back against the end of the bath. She pushed herself up between his legs and settled her body back against his chest, her eyes closed. His hand slipped around her, he gently began to glide his finger tips across her wet skin.

An hour and a half later, they were lying on the bed wrapped in each other's arms, perspiration glistening on their naked bodies. She snuggled into him.

"So much for behaving yourself."

"I think you are as much to blame for that as I am."

"I never said I would behave."

He kissed the top of her head, "You know what; I always felt I had my life sorted and I knew what it was I wanted from it.  I actually thought I was happy. But since I've met you, I've come to realise that I had shut people out. I didn't want to let anyone get close to me. I felt that emotionally I had nothing to offer."

She traced her finger around his nipple, "You certainly proved that theory wrong. To tell you the truth, I felt much the same. After losing Alistair and Rick, I thought I would never really be happy again. You showed me otherwise." Tears pricked her eyes, "And you're so good with Madi, she adores you."

He smiled, "She's hard to resist, just like her mother."

She laughed, "You're a bit of a smooth talker aren't you?"

His lips brushed across her forehead, "I have my moments. By the way, I should warn you that I've got a surprise planned for you and Madi tomorrow."

Adriana glanced up at him, "A warning? I'm not sure I like the sound of that. Do I at least get a hint?"

"Nope, all I'm going to say is that you are going to have to put all your trust in me."

Adriana brows drew together, "I'm not sure if I like surprises."

"As I said, you just have to trust me."

"Please, at least give me a little clue."

"No and that's my final word. You will have to wait until tomorrow when all will be revealed."

She lay her head down on his chest. The steady thrum of his heart echoed in her ears. Her eyes closed; how could she not trust him? Hadn't he already saved her, and not just from drowning?


The morning sun had just begun to creep through the blinds as Hayden nudged Adriana awake.

"I think we had better think about getting up. Madi will be awake soon, and you wouldn't want her walking in on us like this would you?"

Adriana's eyes blinked open as she gazed up at him

sleepily, "You know, that's the first night we have actually slept together."

She placed a light kiss on his cheek, "I could get used to waking up next to you."

His heart clenched "I was just thinking the exact same thing."

Sitting up, she let the sheet drop to her waist. His eyes roamed her body. He reached over and brushed her hair back over her shoulder, exposing her breast.

" I could stay here with you all day."

Her lashes blinked slowly across her eyes, "You and me both, but you're right, Madi will be up any minute."

Reluctantly, she slipped out of bed. His eyes followed her every move until she disappeared into the bathroom. He dropped his head back down on the pillow. It was nice not to think about work for a change. When he was with her she consumed his every thought. How had he managed to fall in love with her so fast? He was normally so cautious when it came to women.

Fifteen minutes later she exited the bathroom, wrapped in one of the hotel robes. He pushed himself up the bed, and rested against the headboard, unable to draw his eyes away from her. She walked over to the dresser. Letting her robe drop to the floor she began to dress. A slight smile touched his lips, knowing he would never tire of seeing her naked. When she had finished dressing, she grabbed a clean towel off the rail and threw it at him.

"Your turn, shower now."

He leapt off the bed and grabbed hold of her, "Thank you

for last night.”

She smiled “My pleasure.”

He took her lips in his. She  responded willingly, jumping away when the door handle rattled. “Shower now,” she snapped.

He saluted, “yes M’am,” he replied, quickly making his way to the bathroom and quietly pulling the door closed behind him. Her eyes scanned the room; would Madison notice there was only one bed? Before she could think anymore about it the door swung open.

“Good morning sweetheart. You slept late.”

Madison rubbed her eyes, as she shuffled into the room. Adriana picked her up and gave her a hug, “Did you have fun yesterday, baby?”

Madison nodded. “How about we order some breakfast and surprise Hayden when he gets out of the shower?” Placing Madison down on the bed Adriana walked over and retrieved the breakfast menu off the table. “What do you feel like? We could have cereal and fresh fruit and toast or sausages, eggs and hash browns. There’s bagels, now I know you like them. To drink we have orange or apple juice. There is chocolate milk or water.”

Madison stared blankly at her. Adriana smiled, “I’ll tell you what. Why don’t we order two of everything, then we can all share?” Madison smiled, nodding her head.

Hayden walked out of the bathroom with a towel slung low around his hips. A loud knock came at the door. He glanced over at Adriana, “Are you expecting anyone?”

“I took the liberty of ordering breakfast. I hope you don’t

mind?" He walked over and opened the door, and watched as two fully laden trolleys were wheeled into the room.

"Your breakfast, sir; now will that be all?" Hayden looked at the quantity of food.

"Yes, more than enough thanks," he replied, giving Adriana a questioning glance.

"Could you wait just a minute?" Hayden walked over to his discarded trousers and pulled a few notes out of the pocket, He placed them in the man's palm.

"Thank you sir, madam," he said, nodding at Adriana as he backed out of the room, closing the door behind him.

"I'm not sure any of us are going to be able to move after eating this lot."

Adriana laughed, "Sorry, Madi and I couldn't decide."

They ate breakfast together. Afterwards Adriana took Madison into the other room to get dressed, while Hayden did the same.

Madison and Adriana walked back into the room. Hayden smiled.

"So, are we all ready for the surprise?"

Adriana eyed him suspiciously, "I'd still feel a lot happier if I knew what it was."

"I like surprises," giggled Madison.

"There see? You'll be fine, I promise."

"We'll see. Come on then, let's go and get this over and done with, the suspense is killing me."

Madison grabbed Hayden's hand, "Come on, hurry."

Hayden smiled, "Women, nag, nag, nag."

"Oh believe me, you haven't heard me nag yet."

"It will give me something to look forward to."

"I could start right now, if you feel like you're missing out."

He grinned, "No, no, I can wait. Now come on, let's get a move on."  They all got into the truck and headed off toward the marina.

# Chapter Sixteen

Adriana gripped the hand rail tightly. Her body shook as she looked down at the rows of yachts and launches  lined up against the wooden jetty. Her hands were damp with perspiration and her heart was pounding in her chest.

"Please, Hayden, anything but this. I can't."

He had expected a little resistance but what he saw in her eyes was pure terror. However, he was determined to help her move past her fear. He picked Madison up.

"Come on, I promise it's perfectly safe." Hayden started to make his way along the wharf.

"Hayden, come back. Please don't make me do this."

He glanced back over his shoulder, "I told you, you have to trust me. I won't  let  anything  happen to you or Madison."

"I don't believe you. No one can promise that." A hard knot formed in her stomach. "Please Hayden, bring her back. You have no right to do this."

He waved his hand at her, signalling for her to follow, "I have faith in you Adriana, you can do this."

Her body was rigid with tension as she watched them slowly make their way along the jetty.

"Mommy's not coming," said Madison, sounding a little concerned. He stopped and looked back. "She will, you wait and see."

Holding her breath Adriana took a tentative step out onto the jetty. It rocked slightly under her weight. Clutching at the railing, she peered over the edge. The water lapped against the large wooden piles that secured the jetty in place. Dark shadows hung around the base of the jetty making the water look black and unforgiving. Her body gave a quick shiver. The sound of the lapping water grated on her nerves. The wharf swayed ever so slightly. She let out a startled gasp, gripping the rail even tighter. When she did glance back up, both Hayden and Madison were standing a little further down the jetty, watching her.

"Hayden please, don't make me do this."

"I'm not making you do anything. You are quite welcome to stay on dry land. I'll take Madison out for a cruise around the harbour."

Madison squealed with delight, clapping her little hands together. Adriana's jaw clenched.

"You will not."

His eyes met hers, "All you have to do is trust me. I won't let anything happen to you, I promise."

"The sea doesn't care that you made some promise to me."

She edged further along the jetty.

"We are not going out in some little runabout."

As she drew closer he stepped off the main jetty onto a smaller one that ran out between two impressive looking launches. Her eyes were focused on her feet as she slowly inched her way forward. When she glanced up, they had disappeared. Anger washed over her. How dare he use her daughter this way? She shuffled along, picking up the pace a little. Her hand was still clutching tightly at the rail. When she saw the narrow jetty ahead of her, she nearly turned back. There was no handrail to cling to. If he hadn't taken Madison, she would have turned and left without another thought. She looked down the length of the jetty, but couldn't see either Hayden or Madison.

"Madison., Madison where are you?" she called, with a note of desperation in her voice.

Madison's head popped over the railings of the launch to Adriana's right. She gave a deep sigh of relief.

"Mommy come quick, look at this."

Adriana took a deep breath and hurried along the jetty. As she neared the launch Hayden's hand appeared through the gap in the side of the launch. Her hand clasped around his. She  gripped on desperately as he  helped her  step aboard. The minute she was safely aboard, she shook loose of his grip and stood glaring at him. "How dare you use Madison like that? You had no right." Her breathing began to settle as she glanced around her.  He was right it certainly wasn't a little runabout.

He gave an apologetic smile. "I'm sorry, but I didn't know any other way to get you aboard, apart from throwing you over my shoulder and carrying you kicking and screaming."

Her eyes narrowed, "You're lucky you didn't."

He took her hand in his, "If I promise never to do anything like that again, will you forgive me?"

She turned her face away, it was impossible to stay mad at him. "So I take it this is my surprise. I can see why you didn't want to tell me."

He dropped her hand and closed the opening between the rails where she had entered.

"What do you think you're doing?"

"We're going out," he said, waving his hand in the general direction of the harbour."

Her hands went to her hips, "We're what?"

He grinned and turned toward the bridge, "We're going out."

She grabbed Madison's hand and pulled her along behind her, as she followed him into the cabin. "We are not going anywhere."

He smiled, as he turned the key and the engine roared to life.

"Why are you doing this? I...can't... "

"I have my reasons."

Her eyes narrowed, "No amount of begging is going to make you change your mind, is it?"

He glanced over at her, "Nope."

She slumped down on one of the chairs. He left her momentarily, as he jumped down onto the lower deck to

release the ropes. The boat drifted backwards. Hayden returned to the cabin, shifted the lever into reverse and gently nudged away from the jetty. Once they were out past the other boats, he headed out through the mouth of the harbour. As soon as they were underway, Adriana felt some of the tension begin to leave her body. He pushed the lever forward, the boat instantly responded. Large wakes rolled out from its bow. He reached down and pulled  out two life jackets and tossed them to Adriana.
"One for you and one for Madi."
Adriana called Madison over and buckled the life jacket on, then slipped hers on and buckled it firmly around her waist.  He motioned for her to come over to him. She turned away, still angry.


        By the time they had reached the open sea, she found she was actually starting to enjoy it. He reached over and grabbed her wrist, pulling her over to him.
"Do you want to drive?"
She tugged against him, "I couldn't possibly."
He laughed, "It's easier than driving a car."
She took the wheel in her hands. "How do you know which way to go?"
He stood behind her, and pointed across to the headlands, "See that point?  Well we want to go around it." His finger moved across slightly "See that beacon? That needs to stay to our left. Do you think you can manage that? " She nodded as her hands tightened on the wheel. He wrapped his arms around her waist.
"I'm still mad at you."

"If this is mad I think I can handle it."

She elbowed him in the ribs. "Don't think you're off the hook."

He smiled "I wouldn't dream of it."

He spent the day showing her along the coastline. They pulled into one of the bays and took the dingy ashore, so they could have a picnic on the beach. It was late afternoon before they returned to the boat. He started it up and headed further up the coast. Adriana was standing at the wheel, Hayden had his arms wrapped around her waist. Madi was busy playing on the floor with some shells she had collected from the beach. As they rounded the point and headed further up the coast, an uneasiness began to creep over her.

"Where are we going?"

He saw the uncertainty in her face, "I told you, you have to trust me."

"I do, but you know full well what this part of the coast means to me."

He looked down at her, his eyes soft, "Yes I do. That's why I bought you out here."

He felt her body tense as the lighthouse came into view. Her hands dropped from the wheel. He reached around her and took control, his arms trapping her there. Tears stung her eyes, "I can't be here."

He kissed her lightly on the top of the head, and turned the boat towards the shore. Adriana couldn't take her eyes off the spot where they had found her husband's yacht. The images they had shown on television came flooding back. The battered yacht had  been almost unrecognizable as it clung precariously to the rocks. She ducked under his arms and moved to the railing, as a sudden wave of nausea washed over her. At the time of the accident it had been hard for her to accept the fact that they were gone forever. She had never really had a chance to say goodbye. Her hands gripped the railing as she stood staring out at the coastline, expecting to see the last remnants of the yacht still clinging to the rocks. Hayden came up behind her and slipped his arms around her waist. There was no strength left in her to fight him.

"Why did you bring me here?"

He was quiet for a minute, "To give you the chance to say goodbye."

Tears trickled down her cheeks, "I can't. If I do, I have to admit they're gone..., forever."

"It's been two years Adriana. It's time to let them go." He clutched her tighter against him, "You need to let go of the guilt you've been carrying around inside you."

She was about to protest when Madison walked up beside them. "Mommy's crying."

Hayden released her so she could crouch down beside her daughter.

"I'm a little sad that's all. This is where your daddy and brother drowned."

Madison took her mother's hand, "Are they still here Mommy?"

A lump formed in Adriana's throat as she looked at her daughter.

"Yes, baby, they are." Adriana pointed over to the rocks, "That's where they found your daddy's boat."

"Are they in hev..in?"

Adriana smiled "Yes baby they are, and they are probably smiling down at us right now."

They both stood at the railing, looking out over the water as the sun slowly slipped down below the horizon. A soft pinkish glow settled across the sky. Hayden moved below deck. The lighthouse stood like a lone sentry, silhouetted by the setting sun, guarding the rugged untouched coastline, warning those who chose to come near, of the danger lurking beneath the waves. Adriana knew she would hold this moment in her heart forever. This beautiful untamed piece of coastline was their final resting place. As the sun vanished below the horizon, the dusky pink sky turned black. The moonlight glistened across the water. It was a perfect night for her to say goodbye. Hayden came up behind them, carrying two little wooden boats with paper sails. Small glowing lanterns hung from their masts. He gave a tentative smile.

"I thought you might like to set these afloat..., as a last goodbye and to help guide their spirits home."

Madison clapped her hands, "can we Mommy?"

Adriana nodded, a fresh flood of tears beginning to flow down her cheeks. Hayden carried Madison's, and he placed the other in Adriana's hand. He guided them to the back of the boat. They both crouched down on the platform together. Hayden gave Madison the boat, while Adriana placed hers into the water, and helped Madison do the same.

"I'm sorry. Goodbye, I'll love you always," she whispered, as she slipped her wedding ring from her finger and placed it in the bottom of the little wooden boat. Adriana pushed hers out to sea, and Madison gave hers a little push whilst Hayden hung onto her top to stop her falling in. Madison gave a delighted little squeal as they watched the boats sail out into the night. The glow of the lanterns shone brightly against the deep dark water. They caught in the current and slowly drifted away, their lanterns growing ever dimmer as they drifted further and further away. Adriana strained to watch them until finally they disappeared from sight. She stood staring out at the darkness. Turning her tear stained face to his, she smiled, "Thank you."

His eyes sought hers, "Take all the time you need. I'll take Madi back inside."

He took Madison by the hand, "Come on, how would you like to steer the boat?"

"Yes please," Madison squealed.

Adriana watched them disappear into the cabin. Her eyes drifted back to the ocean. The little boats had long since disappeared. "I will always love you," she whispered into the darkness.

When she returned to the cabin, Madison was happily perched on Hayden's knee. Her little hands were clasped tightly around the wheel and she had a look of total concentration etched on her face. Adriana smiled; maybe Madison would get to have a father after all; only time would tell. The motor started up. She took one last look towards the coast, then turned back to watch her daughter. Her heart clenched; Hayden would make a wonderful father. She wondered now why she had ever doubted him. He glanced up and caught her watching them. He gave her a knowing look. She wiped away her tears. There was certainly no doubt in her mind that he was the  man  she wanted to spend the rest of her life with. She gave him a tentative smile, "You'll be pleased to know I'm not mad anymore."

"I'm glad to hear it."

"Thank you" she whispered.

He pulled her against him, "You're welcome."

"You have managed to do what no one else could."

His eyes darkened, She elbowed him in the ribs, "Not that, I  meant  giving  me the opportunity to say my goodbyes."

He smiled, "I was just teasing. I knew what you meant." Her eyes sought his. "I'm so lucky to have found you."

"If memory serves me right, it was me that found you. So that makes me the lucky one."

# Chapter Seventeen

The next morning Adriana stood at the railing, feeling the gentle rock of the boat as it rode the swell. They had spent the night anchored in a sheltered bay, a little further up the coast. The guilt had finally gone. What Hayden had done for her was beyond words. She glanced back into the cabin. Her body gave a small quiver. He lay on his stomach, his body tangled in the sheets. She smiled as her eyes ran over his exposed buttocks and strong muscular thigh. Having never known such strong emotion, she wasn't sure how she could love him even more, but she did. He had helped her find a way to say goodbye. Tears trickled down her cheeks. She turned back to the ocean. Was it too good to last? Would she again have to feel the pain of loss? His hands slid around her waist as he pressed his naked body against hers.

"Good morning, Beautiful."

They stood locked together gazing out at the ocean, her body melting against his.

"No regrets?" he asked.

"I have to keep pinching myself to make sure I'm not dreaming."

He kissed the side of her neck, "Believe me, it's no dream."

"Thank you."

"What for?"

"For giving me back my life."

"My pleasure," he kissed her neck. "You know I'd like nothing more than to take you back to bed and make love to you again and again. It pains me to say that we have to leave. It will be high tide soon and I need to take the boat back in."

She snuggled against him. "Just a few more minutes, please. It's so peaceful out here."

"What would you like for breakfast?"

Adriana stomach churned at the thought of food. "I think I'll give breakfast a miss. I'll have something a little later on, when we are on dry land."

He grinned, "Haven't quite got your sea legs yet?"

"No, I'm sure I'll come right once we're off the water."

"You and Madi go ahead. I'll go and take a quick shower." His brow creased.

"You sure you're okay?"

"Of course, why wouldn't I be? Now go ..eat."

She followed him into the cabin. He dressed, then gave her a quick kiss and headed to the galley.

Entering the bathroom, she closed the door behind her. An uneasy feeling crept over her as she counted back the weeks in her head. She was late. Leaning over the sink, she swallowed back the sudden urge to vomit.

"Not now. Please," she said whispered to herself.


Hayden looked up as she approached the table.

"Are you sure you're okay? You look very pale."

Adriana gave him a weak smile, "I'm fine, really." Her stomach lurched at the smell of his cooked breakfast.

A frown crept onto his brow. Her stomach contracted again. "I'll go and start packing while you finish breakfast."

She hurried into the bedroom, and slumped down on the bed. Her head dropped into her hands. After a couple of deep breaths, the nausea passed. Rising to her feet, she lifted the suitcase up off the floor, placed it on the bed and began to pack up her things. Her instincts told her she was pregnant and she knew exactly when conception had taken place. All she wanted to do now was get home, and confirm what she already knew. If her fears proved to be correct, then she would have some very serious decisions to make. Why now? They had only been seeing each other for a few months. What would he think? That she had done this on purpose, just to get her hands on his money? Her stomach tightened. Hopefully the self diagnosis was wrong. Her hand went to her abdomen. Having a baby with him wouldn't be the worst thing that could happen, but the timing certainly could have been better.

Once back on dry land they packed the car and headed home. The drive was quiet. Adriana spent most of the time staring out the window. She jumped with fright when he placed his hand on her knee.

"Are you sure you're okay?"

She turned to look at him and forced a smile. "Just tired. Someone kept me up most of the night," she said, trying to make light of it.

He grinned, "Sorry,", he glanced in the rear view mirror at the  sleeping Madison. "I was having trouble keeping my hands to myself."

"I noticed," she placed her hand on top of his, "Don't ever be sorry for that."

He smiled but it didn't quite  reach his eyes. His gut sensed there was something wrong.

When they finally drew up in front of the house, she sat there for a minute, staring up at the front door. There was no  way she  would burden her mother with another child in the house. Hayden helped her inside with their bags. Madison hurried off to find her grandmother. Adriana walked back out on the porch with him, wondering if a baby would change things between them. She wrapped her arms around his neck.

"Thank you for everything. Most men wouldn't have bothered."

He kissed the tip of her nose, "You're welcome."

Her eyes moistened, "Thank you again."

"Get some rest, you look exhausted. I'll ring you tomorrow."

Adriana watched him walk back down the path, hoping it wouldn't be for the last time.

The next morning she sat in the Doctor's surgery in nervous anticipation, as she waited for her results.

Dr Jacobs walked back into the room. "Well Adriana, I'm pleased to say you are most definitely pregnant."

She gave him a weak smile.

"That wasn't quite the reaction I was expecting" he said, his brow creasing.

"Oh, no it's fine really. Just a little unexpected that's all."

He smiled, "Planned or not, in about seven month's time you will be having a baby."

"I know, and I'm happy really," she hesitated. "I'm just not sure the father will be. You see we haven't been together that long. This will come as quite a surprise."

"Well, I'll give you some advice from a male's perspective. The sooner the better. It won't get any easier, the longer you wait. There is never the perfect time for this sort of thing."

She nodded rising to her feet, "Well, thank you. No doubt I'll be seeing you sometime soon."

He held open the door for her, "Take care Adriana, and remember what I said. The sooner the better."

As she walked out of the doctor's surgery, she knew she had to tell him now, before she had time to think about it and come up with a million excuses why not to.

Her mother glanced up as Adriana entered the store. "Did you get what you needed to, done?"

"What? Oh, yes, yes I did."

Her mother looked a little harder at her. "Are you alright? You look a little pale."

She gave her mother a tentative smile, "I'm fine Mom, honestly. It's been a busy weekend, that's all."

Her mother smiled, "I like him."

"Who? What? Oh, Hayden. Sure, he's great."

Her mother frowned, "I've got some news that might cheer you up. Leslie came in this morning, and renewed her contract. And another woman rang to say she would call in later on today, to see you about selling her products through the store."

Adriana tried to appear interested, "That's great." So he had sorted it out, as he promised. Always true to his word.

"Thanks for watching the store, I really appreciate it. There is something else I needed to see too. Would it be possible for you to stay on a bit longer? It won't take long, I promise."

Patricia's brow creased, "Of course, as long as you're back in time for me to pick up Madison from Pre-School."

"I'll only be a half an hour or so. I just need to make a quick phone call first."

Her mother looked at her questioningly , "Are you sure there's nothing wrong?"

Adriana forced a smile. "Worrying as usual. Honestly Mom I'm fine."

She headed into the back office and closed the door behind her. Picking up the phone she punched in the number.

"Hello, Radcliff's, Joanne speaking. How can I help you?"

Adriana hesitated, "Hi Joanne. I was wondering if it would be possible to speak with Hayden, please."

"Can I ask who's speaking?"

"It's Adriana Richards. It's a personal matter."

"Oh I see. Well, I'm afraid he's in a meeting with a client at the moment. He has quite a lot on today. Would you like me to get him to call you when he's free?"

"Yes, umm, on second thoughts no. I would actually like to see him if that's at all possible? I only need a few minutes of his time."

"Well, he does have an opening at about eleven thirty, but I'm not sure if I should use it for personal..."

"Please, he won't mind, I promise you."

The phone went quiet, "Umm okay, as long as you're out by the time his next client arrives."

"I will be, and thank you. There is just one other thing. Please don't let him know I'm coming."

"Oh, no..., I couldn't possibly. I could get fired."

"Please, it's a surprise."

"I'm sorry, I'm new to the job. I'll have to make sure I'm allowed to do that. If you wait just a minute I'll check."

"Sure," Adriana heard the phone being put down on the desk. A few minutes later she came back, "That's fine; we'll see you at eleven thirty."

"Thank you, I really appreciate it."

Hayden sat gazing out the window. The last

client had irritated him a little and the thought of yet another board meeting didn't help to lift his mood. He glanced at the clock. The  board meeting  wasn't  for another  thirty minutes. He thought about nipping out to see Adriana but knew if he did he wouldn't want to come back. He glanced  up  as  the  door  opened.  A  deep frown  instantly creased  his brow.

"Jessica, what are you doing here?"

She smiled seductively, "I was just visiting with your mother, and I thought I would take the opportunity to say hello." Her short skirt rode up her tanned shapely thighs as she crossed the  room  towards him. His  eyes  were momentarily drawn to the short hem line.

"I've told you before. I'm not interested."

She perched herself on  the edge of the desk, giving him a clear  view right up her  skirt, to her lace  panties. Her deliciously full lips pouted as her smooth leg brushed against his arm. Her startling blue eyes met with his.

"Can't  we  let  bygones  be  bygones, and  at  least  be friends?"

He went to stand and she pushed him back down.

"Jessica, I don't know what the hell it is you are playing at, but I don't have time for this." Placing her hands down on the desk she leant back, deliberately pushing her bust forward. Peaked  taut  nipples  strained  against  her  tight fitting top and he couldn't help but notice she wasn't wearing a bra. His eyes narrowed.

"What do you want, Jessica?"

She gave him a sly smile, "Now Hayden, there's no need to be like that." Getting to her feet she placed her hands on the arms of his chair and leant in, bringing her bust within inches of his face. "I thought the reason for my visit would be rather obvious."

He let out an exasperated sigh, "We've have been through this already. I don't want you. How much plainer can I make it?"

She swivelled his chair so that his back was to the door. "Am I not good enough for you? Is that it?" Her fingers raked through his hair. "I could make you very happy."

He swatted her hands away, as she stepped across his outstretched legs. Her skirt rode up high on her thighs. His eyes turned cold, as he reached up to grip her hips preventing her from depositing herself in his lap.

"Oh Hayden, come on. You know you like it."

At that moment Jessica glanced up to see a horrified Adriana standing in the open doorway. Jessica grinned at her "Do you like what you see, baby?"

Before he could answer, Jessica lowered her lips to his. Adriana had seen more than enough.

Backing out of the room, she turned and ran for the elevator. Her finger pressed down on the button and she didn't release it until she heard the ping informing her it had arrived. Fighting back the tears, she stepped in and waited for the doors to close. What an idiot she had been. Of course she wasn't the only woman in his life. Look at him; women simply drooled over him. Her back stiffened; well from now on, this one wouldn't be. She swiped impatiently at the tears now trickling down her cheeks. How could he have been so caring and thoughtful to her face and such a lying bastard when she wasn't watching.

Hayden shoved Jessica away. It was obvious the soft approach wasn't going to work.

"What the hell are you playing at? Get out of my office."

She straightened her skirt, smiling inwardly to herself. "Come on Hayden. It was only a little bit of harmless fun."

He jaw tensed as he got to his feet, "Do you see me laughing?"

Placing her hand on his chest she gave him a doleful look. He grabbed her arm, walked her to the door and virtually threw her out of his office. He looked past her to the receptionist, "Don't you dare let this woman in here again."

The receptionist nodded.

"Did you hear me?"

"Yes, sir."

"Good, now see to it that she's escorted out, and make sure they never let her back in here..., ever!"

"Hayden come on. Don't you think you're overreacting just a little?"

"When it comes to you Jessica, no I don't."

He turned from her and re entered his office, slamming the door closed behind him. He walked over to the window, still fuming with anger. Why had she come here? He had made it perfectly clear months ago, that he didn't want anything to do with her. His fists balled. It had his interfering mother written all over it. There was a knock at the door.

"What?" he yelled.

The door opened, "Umm, Sir, the board is waiting on you."

"Tell them I'll be there in a minute."

"Yes sir," she replied, backing out of the room.

He took a couple of deep calming breaths as he headed down towards the board room. What he had planned wasn't going to sit well with his mother, but it was long overdue. He strode into the  room, his mouth set in a firm line. Everyone was present except his mother. He glanced at his watch, giving an exasperated sigh as he took his seat.

Adriana wiped the tears away. The lift stopped on the next floor, the doors opened and April Radcliff stepped in. She gave Adriana a patronizing smile.

"Good morning Adriana, how nice to see you. I'm glad I have run into you actually. I wanted a quiet word."

Adriana's body tensed.

"Just between the two of us, you understand."

Adriana didn't have the emotional strength to argue. If she had been anywhere else, she would have simply walked away.

"What do you want now? Why can't you just leave me the hell alone?"

April smiled, "I will my dear..., as soon as you stop seeing my son."

Even though she had no intention of seeing Hayden again, it still angered her that this woman thought she could manipulate people's lives.

"I think your son is old enough to decide that for himself, don't you?" Adriana stiffened as she recalled the scene in the office. Yes, he certainly had the freedom to choose to see whomever he liked.

April smiled, fully aware of what Adriana had just witnessed. "I have no idea why he is interested in the likes of you, but I'm warning you now, stay away from him. He is way out of your league. You said it yourself."

Adriana fists clenched, "You may have control over your son, but don't think for a minute that you can tell me what to do. If I want to see Hayden, I will."

"Well in that case, you leave me with no other choice. If you keep seeing him I will disinherit him. He will have nothing. All his hard work over the past few years, his siblings will benefit from. I wish him to marry a woman of my choosing. If he is to have any future with this family or this company, he will do as I ask."

Adriana's jaw dropped open, "You would do that to your own son? Doesn't his happiness mean anything to you?"

April gave her a smug look, "Yes I would. As for his 'happiness', I find the emotion very over rated. It would be for his own good. He will thank me in the end. Now be a good girl and run along. Go and find some other poor unsuspecting victim to suck money out of."

The lift door opened and April stepped out. Adriana stood dumbfounded. How could anyone be so unfeeling to their own child? She stepped forward and held the door open, "You know what April? I should hate you, but honestly, I feel sorry for you."

April grinned, "Oh and why would that be?"

"Because you don't have the ability to love. One day, your children are going to wake up to your meddling ways and you will be all alone."

April went quiet.

Adriana burst into tears the minute the doors closed. How could she have let herself get pregnant to a man who obviously wasn't ready for any sort of commitment? And to think that he loved her was a joke. He was a Radcliff after all. He had seemed so perfect. Maybe that was her mistake. There was no such thing as the 'perfect man'. Luckily, she had found out now. Him and his family had brought her nothing but pain and heartache and she didn't care if she never saw any of them again.

# Chapter Eighteen

Tears streamed down her cheeks. People stared as she passed, but she was beyond caring. She walked into the local park and slumped down on the wooden bench. Her heart clenched as she gazed across the park. A family of four were happily playing on the swings. Her head dropped into her hands. At times, it had been quite a struggle to raise Madison on her own and now she would have to do it all over again. How could she face her mother, knowing what a stupid mistake she had made? She had lost her heart to a man who didn't know how to love.

A shadow fell over her.

"Adriana.... Whatever is the matter?"

Tilting her head up, she  saw Ross standing in front of her, a  deep  frown etched into his brow. Guilt clutched at her;

she had abandoned him so easily. He dropped down onto the seat beside her, and slipped his arm around her waist. Emotionally drained, she rested her head on his shoulder.

"Come on Adriana, it can't be that bad."

"Oh Ross, I've made such a mess of things. I don't know what I'm going to do."

Ross gave her a gentle squeeze, "Why don't you tell me what's upset you?  Maybe I can help."

She pushed away from him. "I couldn't, not after what I did to you. Why would you want to? You were there for me when I needed a friend. When Hay... he came along I simply forgot about you. I don't deserve your help."

"Because I care about you, that's why. I have to admit though, it tore me up inside to see you with him, I'm man enough to admit it. I'm just not sure what you were thinking. Of all the men you could choose, you had to go and pick him."

"Ross, I'm so sorry."

"Don't sweat it. We all make mistakes."

Silence settled between them.

"I thought he loved me. It turns out I was wrong... He's been seeing other women behind my back. On top of that, his mother hates me and has threatened to disinherit him if I continue seeing him. Not that I ever want to see him again." She shook her head slowly from side to side. "It's all such a big mess."

"How could he do that to you? I should go over there and sort him out, once and for all."

She grabbed at his arm, "No, I think it's better this way.

I'll make a clean break. He never actually said we were exclusive, I just assumed we were. Now I realise how stupidly naive I was."

Ross hugged her, "You're not stupid or naive. Haven't you heard the saying, 'love is blind'? If anything, he's the stupid one. If he can't see how lucky he was to have both you and Madison, then it's his loss. He doesn't deserve you."

Guilt weighed heavily upon her. How could she have been such an idiot, was she was so blind that she couldn't see a good thing when it was staring her right in the face?

"I've been so insensitive toward you. I never realised how it felt to love someone who didn't love you back. Now I know what it must have been like for you."

"You can't help who you fall in love with. I'm just glad to be a part of your life. Oh no, did I just say that? It sounded so tragic."

Adriana laughed, "Actually I thought it sounded rather sweet."

She gave him a little kiss on the cheek, "Thank you."

He smiled "Anytime, now how about we get you a cup of coffee and settle you down a bit?" He took her hand and drew her to her feet. Placing her arm through his, they walked towards the cafe. He took the liberty of ordering for her. They slipped into one of the corner booths. She caught his eyes from across the table, "I didn't mean to lay this on you. All I seem to do lately, is burden you with my problems. I didn't even keep my promise. I should have told you I was seeing someone."

Ross patted her hand, "Actually, I had been trying to catch up with you. I wanted to warn you about him. He's a womanizer Adriana, everybody knows that."

Her eyes moistened, "I'd heard the rumours. I just chose to ignore them. That'll teach me. Well believe me, I certainly know now."

"So what are you going to do? Have you told him you don't want to see him anymore?"

She sipped her coffee. "No. I can't. I don't even want... to see him again." The words caught in her throat. "He'll make up some excuse, and I'll want to believe him. I'm worried I could actually consider giving him another chance." She placed her mug back down on the table. "What if he comes to the store? I won't be able to resist him, I know it."

"Do you want me to have a word with him? Warn him off"

Her eyes widened, "No! No, I couldn't expect that of you. I'll have to be strong and tell him it's over. He won't believe it coming from you."

"Maybe you should go away for a bit, give things time to settle."

Adriana frowned, "I couldn't."

"Give me one good reason why not?"

"Well, there's the store, for one."

"Come on Adriana, you'll have to do better than that. You know full well that your mother will watch it for you."

A wide grin broke out across Ross's face, "I've just had a brilliant idea. We could go away on holiday together. For a couple of weeks until this all blows over. It'll give you time to sort things out. The plus side would be, not having to face him right away."

"What about Madi?"

"She can come with us. Come on. I'm due a holiday. My brother is always insisting he can watch the store for me."

She was more than tempted, but knew that it wasn't going to blow over. In approximately seven months' time she would be having his baby. "If I say yes, it would be just as friends. Is that understood? I couldn't possibly...."

Ross took her hand "And I wouldn't expect you to. What do you take me for? Come on, it will be fun. You would be doing me a huge favour. Who wants to go on holiday by themselves?"

"So how long are we talking?"

"We could make it as long or as short as you want. My uncle has a holiday house up at Seven Tree Pond. It would be beautiful up there this time of year. He won't be using it as he's over in Australia on business."

"Sounds perfect. If I did say yes, could we leave tomorrow?"

"I'm sure I could arrange that."

The tension began to ease, it wasn't a solution but at least it would give her a little time to decide what she was going to do.

Ross got to his feet. "I'll walk you back to the store. It shouldn't take me long to organise things with my brother."

Her eyes moistened.

"Adriana, are you sure about this?"
She nodded. It wasn't like she was running away.
Ross saw her to the door of the store. "I'll ring you later
and let you know how it's all going."
"That would be great, and thanks again."
He grinned, "My pleasure."


Her mother looked up as she entered. "What's
got you looking so serious?"
"Nothing. Mom..., I need to ask you something."
"Fire away."
"Would you be interested in looking after the store for a
little while? A couple of weeks maybe?" Her mother's
eyebrows rose, "Why, is something the matter?"
"No..., I just I feel  I need to get away for a bit. A holiday
of sorts."
"I think that's a great idea. Are you going with Hayden?"
Adriana's eyes moistened, "No! I'm not." she snapped
back, "We are going on holiday with Ross."
"Ross? I don't understand. When you say 'we' I presume
you mean Madi and you?"
"Yes. Look Mom, I'm sorry, but I'm just not in a fit state
to talk about it right now."
"I thought things were going well with you and
Hayden?"
Adriana shook her head, "So did I. Please, can we just
drop this. I'll tell you everything I promise, just not now...
So can you watch the store or not?"
"Of course I will, you know that. Can I at least ask where
you're going?"

"I'd rather not say. That way you won't have to lie if Hayden comes around looking for me. I'll have my cell phone with me. You can call whenever you want. I'll be sure to ring you when we get there, so you know we have arrived safely."

Her mother looked a little sceptical. "I'm fine, Mom honest."

"Do you think it wise to go on holiday with Ross? What will Hayden think?"

"Hayden can think what he damn well likes. I don't really care. Now please, can we just leave it at that? I'll explain everything when I get back. I promise."

Adriana crossed the store and entered the office, closing the door behind her. She leant back against the door. Her hand moved to her abdomen. "I'm sorry. Don't worry, everything will be okay" she whispered softly to the baby growing inside her.

Hayden would have made a wonderful father, but would he want anything to do with this baby? Tears trickled down her cheeks. At times he could be so caring. That's what made his deceit so hard to accept. She drew in a deep sobering breath. Hadn't she had managed on her own before? Surely she could do it again if she really had to. Maybe it was better this way. If his mother ever found out she was pregnant, she would disinherit him. Not that it was any of her concern anymore. Maybe she could pass the baby off as Ross's and save everyone a lot of heartache.

A soft knock sounded on the door. "Adriana, is it

alright if I head off now and pick up Madi?"

Adriana opened the door, "Sure, I'll be fine. We can talk at home."

Her mother's eyes softened when she saw Adriana's pale drawn face.

"Before you ask, I'm fine, honestly." Adriana placed her hand on her mother's arm. "Please just go and pick up Madi."

Her mother drew her into her arms. Adriana had to fight to keep the tears away. When she pulled away, her eyes were glistening. Patricia turned to leave, "I'll see you at home then?"

Adriana nodded. Patricia left, closing the door behind her. Adriana's stomach contracted as she made an urgent dash to the bathroom. Taking a few deep breaths, she let herself relax against the wall and waited for her stomach to settle. It was going to be near to impossible to hide her pregnancy from Ross, but she wasn't ready to tell anyone just yet. Not until she had had time to think things through. She stumbled out of the bathroom and collapsed into the chair. Her cell phone rang. Her heart clenched when she saw it was Hayden. Her finger hovered over the answer button. Just as she was about to push it, the ringing stopped. It would be a huge mistake to speak to him now while she was in such a distressed state. Who knows what she would agree to? Ross was right, she needed time.

Hayden walked out of the Boardroom with a deep frown etched on his brow. He rubbed his forehead. After two long hours of debating, he had managed to convince the Board to remove his mother's influence from the day to day running of the mill. He hadn't wanted it to be this way, but she had forced his hand. He couldn't have her manipulating the workers and their families. His mother had kicked up such a fuss, accusing them all of conspiring against her. The meeting had ended with her storming from the room, refusing to ever set foot in the building again. April had always been one for theatrics, and he would bet his life on it that she would be back in a day or two. Her seat on the Board still remained. Even though she was no longer chair woman, she still had some control over the company's finances. As for the personnel, they were all now under Hayden's authority. His mother had lost the ability to meddle in the employee's lives. As the years passed, he had watched her become more and more bitter. Was it past resentment that had made her this way? His father had always put the business before his wife and family. Hayden shrugged his shoulders. Whatever the reason, one thing was certain, the company was going to run a lot smoother without her at the helm.

Derek slapped his hand down on Hayden's shoulder, "I didn't know you had it in you. Going up against Mother like that. You're lucky it didn't all blow up in your face."

Hayden's eyes narrowed, "If the Board hadn't backed me, I would have resigned."

His brother stopped mid stride, "You're pulling my leg right?"

"I've always fancied having my own business, starting it

up from scratch."

Derek roared with laughter, "Doing what exactly? A gigolo perhaps?"

Hayden's eyes turned cold, "Landscaping actually."

Derek punched him in the arm "I can see it now. My brother, sweating behind a shovel."

Hayden smiled, realising his brother didn't really know him at all.

"Well I'm glad you didn't. I'd hate to see you fail."

"I don't fail."

"I suppose I would have to agree with that. You know you are more like Father than you realise."

Hayden's jaw clenched, "I'm nothing like him. Today proves that."

Derek held his hands up, "Fine, whatever you say."

"Hey, I meant to ask. What's happening with that little bit of arse you've been tapping?" He clicked his fingers, trying to remember her name. "That's it, Adria...."

He didn't have time to finish, as he felt the power of Hayden's fist drive into his stomach. He crumpled to the floor. Hayden stood over him, his fist still tightly clenched, "Don't you ever speak about her like that again."

Derek let out a groan.

"Is that clear?"

"Geez, message received." Derek replied, clutching at his stomach. "You could've just said, 'shut the hell up'."

Hayden grinned, "You're getting soft in your old age. A few years ago you would have taken it and thrown one back."

Hayden  reached out his hand to help his brother to his feet.

"You took me by surprise, that's all. So you're serious about this girl then?"

"Oh, I'm serious alright. I'm thinking I might ask her to marry me."

Derek's mouth dropped open, "I never thought I'd see the day that I'd hear those words coming from your mouth."

Hayden grinned, "Me neither."


Feeling absolutely exhausted, Adriana dragged herself through the front door.

Her mother came up the hall to meet her.

"Adriana, you look terrible."

Adriana gave her a strained smile "Thanks."

"Why don't you go and lie down for a bit. I'll call you when dinner's ready."

"I'm not hungry, Mom. I just need sleep."

Her mother went to insist, but looking at her daughter's pale drawn face, thought better of it.

"Go on up. I'll check on you a little later to see if we can't get you to eat something."

Adriana nodded as she slowly climbed the stairs. She collapsed  onto her bed, too weak to even cry, convinced it was karma. Why did she have to go and break her promise? If she had stayed faithful to her husband, she wouldn't be in her present predicament. Her body slipped down the bed. Turning on her side, she curled her body up into a ball. Her eyelids fluttered shut.

When she woke the room was blanketed in darkness. She sat up and reached out to turn the light on. The room swayed a little as she struggled to her feet. Pregnancy had never really been very kind to her. At the end of the second month, she was always hit with a bad run of morning sickness and found it hard to keep anything down. She slowly made her way toward  the door. Her mother had left the hall light on, which meant that Madison was already in bed. Creeping quietly along the hall she pushed  Madison's  door   open.  Her daughter was sound asleep, the  blankets pulled snugly up  around  her  chin. Adriana smiled, as she pulled the door closed and made her way downstairs. As she entered the kitchen her mother glanced up.

"I didn't think you would still be up."

"I had a feeling you might come down. Do you want a cup of tea? The jug has just boiled"

"Thanks, that would be great."

"You still don't look too good."

"I'll be fine. I must have caught a stomach bug or something."

Patricia handed her a cup of hot tea.

"Ross rang while you were asleep. I didn't want to wake you. He said to tell you everything is arranged and he will pick you up at ten."

Adriana focus dropped to the cup in her hand, "Thanks. I suppose I had better get an early night then. I'll pack in the morning."

"I'll give you a hand if you like."

"That would be great, thanks. Well, I'm  going to call it a

night then. I'll see you bright and early in the morning."

"Are you not going to have anything to eat?"

Adriana grabbed a couple of plain biscuits from the cupboard then headed toward the stairs, "Goodnight Mom."

"Is that all you're going to have to eat?"

"My stomach is still a little tender. Thanks for the tea," she called, making a quick exit. When she reached her room she picked up her phone and flipped it open. There were five missed calls, all from Hayden. Her finger stood poised over his number. The phone snapped shut. If she rang him now it would only make matters worse. She finished her tea and biscuits, just managing to keep them both down. Tomorrow she would simply leave all this mess behind.

# Chapter Nineteen

Adriana woke the next morning feeling nauseous. The thought of the long car ride only made her feel worse. Her mother appeared at the bedroom door with a cup of tea and some toast.

"How are you feeling this morning?"

Adriana forced a smile, "Much better."

Her mother raised one eyebrow, "So why don't I believe you? Why don't you postpone this trip for a couple of days, at least until you are feeling a little better. You look terrible."

Adriana gave her a half hearted smile.

"Full of compliments this morning aren't we?"

"I'm thinking of what's best for you and the ba..., Madi. There is nothing wrong with that, is there?."

Adriana eyed her suspiciously, "You know, don't you?"

Her mother nodded, "You should have told me."

"I was going to. I only found out yesterday. I had a few things to think through."

"So when is the baby due?"

"In about seven months from now."

"It's Hayden's, I'm guessing."

"Mom. What do you take me for? Of course it's Hayden's."

Her mother's brow creased, "So why are you running off with Ross. I thought you loved Hayden."

Adriana's eyes moistened, "I do, that's the whole problem. It's not going to work out. I need time to think."

"I don't understand. I thought everything was going so well?"

Adriana shook her head, "So did I, but I've found out he's not the man I thought he was. So if he comes around looking for me, don't tell him anything."

"Adriana, do you really think running away is the answer?"

"I'm not running away. It's a holiday. I just need to get my head around all this. It's the only option I have."

"Fine, I won't say another word. But please be careful and take care of yourself. Have you told Ross about the baby?"

"No and I'm not going to. At least not yet, anyway."

"Don't you think he has a right to know? It's obvious how he feels about you."

Adriana rubbed her throbbing temples, "I know Mom, don't worry, I've already told him we can only ever be friends."

"Even so, I think he deserves to know."

"I will tell him, just not today, okay? I just want to get away from here."

Her mother walked over and pulled  the suitcase off the top shelf in the closet. "Right, so where do I start? You sit and finish your breakfast while I pack." Her mother opened the underwear drawer and pulled out a pair of lace underwear. She quickly placed them back in the drawer, "You certainly won't be needing those."

"Mom..., I appreciate your help, I really do. But I can do my own packing. Why don't you go and get started on Madi's?"

"Oh, right," she pushed the drawer closed.

"Call me if you need a hand." She walked to the door and stopped, "Don't worry, it'll all sort itself out in the end. Just go on your little trip. Relax and enjoy yourself. It'll do you the world of good."

"Thanks Mom."

Her mother left the room. Adriana's shoulders slumped. It was going to be hard work pretending that everything was all right, when it was far from it.


By ten thirty they were all packed and waiting at the door. Madison had asked if Hayden was coming. Adriana found it hard to tell her he wasn't. She had become very attached to him over the past couple of months. Ross pulled up at the curb in a late model Mazda station wagon. He met Adriana at the door as she struggled out of the house with all their luggage.

"Sorry, but Madi wasn't keen on leaving much behind."

Ross looked down at Madison, "It looks like you're moving house Madi, not going on holiday."

Madison didn't seem to hear him as she dragged her little blue suitcase down the stairs. She stood watching as everything was loaded into the back of the car, to ensure nothing of hers would be left behind. Ross forced the back hatch closed, smiling to himself.

"Okay, are we all set?"

"Just a minute," Adriana gasped, as she rushed back into the house and headed for the bathroom.

She wiped her mouth, catching her reflection in the mirror. Her face was pale and her eyes were ringed with dark circles. Pinching her cheeks, she tried in vain to put some colour into them. Hopefully Ross wouldn't notice. Giving a long sigh she turned from the mirror and made her way back outside. Her mother stood on the porch waiting for her.

"Take care, and ring me as soon as you get there."

Adriana kissed her mother's cheek, "Don't worry Mom, I'll be fine. We'll be back before you know it."

Madi waved furiously as they pulled away from the curb and headed down the street. Adriana breathed a little easier when they finally reached the outskirts of town. Thankfully she had managed to avoid bumping into Hayden. Everything was going to be alright. She would make sure of it. For Madison's and the baby's sake. There was new life growing inside her. A new beginning. Secretly she hoped it might be a boy, but if it was a girl she would be equally pleased. Would the child look like Hayden, she glanced over her shoulder; or more like Madi?

Lowering her seat back, she lay there listening to the constant chatter spilling from Madison's mouth as Ross patiently answered all her questions.


Hayden strode into the office, a deep crease across his forehead. He stopped at the reception desk.

"Good morning Hayden," the receptionist said cheerily.

He turned his cold grey eyes on her, "What's good about it. Tell me that?"

"Umm, I...."

He rolled his eyes, "What appointments have I got today?" he snapped impatiently. The young receptionist took the appointment book out of the drawer, accidently dropping it as she did so. He glared at her as he reached down and swiped it up off the floor. Why hadn't Adriana answered his calls? She had seemed a little distracted when he had dropped her and Madi home. He flicked through the book, stopping at yesterday's entries.

"What's this?" he said, putting the book down on the desk in front of her and stabbing his finger at the open page.

She hesitated.

"Umm." She looked down to where he was pointing.

"Adriana..."

"I can read."

"Well, she wanted...."

He thumped his fist down on the book, making her jump, "Spit it out woman! Wanted what?"

"She didn't say what it was about. Some...thing., personal she said."

His eyes narrowed, "So? Did she keep her appointment or not?"

"Well, yes, but...."

"But what?"

"She went to your office, and  came running back a few minutes later, looking rather distressed. The last I saw of her, she was entering the lift."

His brow creased, "Distressed?"

"Yes, in tears."

"And you didn't think to tell me?"

"I thought you had had words."

"What! Don't be so  ridiculous. I would never...." He  glanced down at the entry again. Eleven thirty. He slammed the book closed, "Shit."

The receptionist looked up at him, "Excuse me?"

 He clenched his fists, "Did my mother know she was coming?"

"I'm not sure... She was in here a few times, but I don't remember her looking at the book."

He knew in his gut that what had happened had everything to do with his mother. He cursed under his breath as he strode across the room to the lift. "I'm going out."

"But Mr Radcliff, you have an appointment in ten minutes."

He gave a momentary glance backwards, "Stall them or cancel. I don't care which."

"But Mr Radcliff." The doors closed.  He turned and drove his fist into the wooden panelling, It splintered on impact. Cursing, he withdrew his hand. Pain shot up his arm. Why couldn't his mother stay out of his life? It was obvious why Jessica had paid him that little visit. How much had Adriana seen? He ran the scene through his head and let out a groan. It didn't look good. Jessica had been straddled across his lap with her skirt hoisted to the top of her thighs. He groaned, she had kissed him. He pushed his hand through his hair. The lift came to a stop, the doors opened. He strode over to his vehicle. No wonder she hadn't answered his calls. Hopefully she would give him the chance to explain. If she would trust him enough to believe it was all his mother's doing.

He pulled up in front of the store and slipped out from behind the wheel, slamming the door closed. Drawing in a couple of deep breaths, he tried to calm himself. He glanced down at his grazed knuckles. His jaw tensed as he shoved his injured hand into his pocket. Pushing the door open he entered the store. He stopped short at the sight of Patricia dusting the selves. She turned at the sound of the bell.

"Oh," was the only word she uttered.

His eyes narrowed, "Where is she?"

"Who?"

"I didn't come here to play games. You know damn well who."

"There is no need to be like that; as you can see she's not here."

"So where is she?"

All she said was, she needed to get away for awhile."

He gave an impatient grunt, "Is that all you are going to give me?"

A frown crept across her brow, "It's all I've got. She wouldn't tell me where she was going."

"I need to speak with her."

"Well I'm sorry, but at the moment I know about as much as you do. You could always try her cell phone."

"Don't you think I've already tried that? She won't answer" he snapped back.

"Look, don't you come in here and think you can throw your weight around. Now I've already told you all I know, so if you don't mind, I would prefer it if you left."

He made no move to leave "I'm sorry. I shouldn't be taking it out on you."

"No, you shouldn't."

He shuffled his feet "How long did she say she was going to be gone?"

"Honestly, I'm not exactly sure. Two weeks, maybe three. Who knows?"

"Three weeks! I can't possibly wait that long."

"You might not have a choice."

He turned to leave.

"Hayden, when she rings, is there anything you want me to tell her?"

He turned back "Could you tell her I'm sorry, and it wasn't what it looked like."

Adriana's mother looked at him quizzically, "What wasn't what it looked like?"

He caught her eye, "Just tell her. She'll know what I'm referring to."

Hayden drove back to the office. He didn't feel in the mood for seeing anybody, but right now he needed something else to think about. He stomped through the office, nearly knocking Derek off his feet as he rounded the corner.

"Damn it. Watch where the hell you're going," he snapped.

"What's your problem?" Derek snapped back.

"Nothing."

"I can see that. I don't suppose your foul mood has anything to do with your girlfriend running off with another man?"

Hayden turned, his fists clenched, "I'd advise you to keep your mouth shut."

"Oh  come on. Forget her, move on. It's obvious she has."

Hayden tensed ready to strike, "What in the hell are you talking about?"

"I saw her this morning, plain as day, leaving town with that guy from the ice cream parlour. The car was loaded to the roof. Face it Hayden, it's obvious she has found someone else."

Hayden spun on his heel and strode into his office, slamming the door closed behind him. Minutes later, there was a light tap on the door.

"What!" he yelled at the closed door. The receptionist opened the door cautiously.

"I'm terribly sorry sir, but your appointment is here."

He grunted, "Cancel it."

"But Mr Rad..."

"I said cancel it. Tell them it's  an emergency or

something"

She shook her head as she pulled the door closed. He leaned back in the chair. Was he too late? Had she finally got fed up with all the drama that surrounded him? He wouldn't blame her if she wanted nothing more to do with him. He raked his fingers through his hair. Had his mother finally succeeded?

# Chapter Twenty

Adriana's eyes turned toward the two figures huddled together at the lake edge. The sound of one of Madison's little giggles drifted up towards her. Ross had been so good with her taking her swimming, something Adriana still didn't feel comfortable doing. Over the past few weeks she had come to the realisation that she couldn't put all her fears onto Madison. She smiled to herself. Earlier, Ross had taken Madison out onto the lake in a row boat and tried to teach her how to fish. She gave a little sigh. Though still suffering a little from nausea, the vomiting had subsided and she had actually begun to relax a little. Rising to her feet she headed down to the lake edge.

"What's going on down here?"

Madison squealed as a fish leapt out of the water just off

shore.

"A fish, Mommy, look."

"I can see. And look, there are some more," Adriana said, pointing to a spot a little further to the right. Madison got to her feet and ran along the bank to watch them.

Ross turned to Adriana. "She didn't like me catching a fish on the hook. It really upset her. I had to release it and throw it back."

Adriana laughed, "A bit of her mother has obviously rubbed off on her."

Adriana looked out over the water, "I'll be sorry to leave this place."

He smiled, "I was thinking the very same thing, but we can't hide out here forever. We both have businesses to run. As it is, we have stayed longer than we intended."

Adriana walked over to a nearby log and sat down.

Ross made his way over to her and dropped down beside her. "Madison's a good kid. You have done a great job with her. She's a lot like you, you know." He took her hand. "You're looking better."

She leaned over and placed her head on his shoulder, "All thanks to you."

A comfortable silence settled between them, as they watched Madison playing at the water's edge. Ross kissed her lightly on the top of her head.

"Adriana, why won't you let me look after you?"

She smiled, "Isn't that what you've been doing for the past two and a half weeks?"

"That's not what I meant."

She sat up, pulling her hand from his.

"Ross please, can't we just leave things as they are?"

He stiffened "Why? We get on so well. We could make it work, I'm sure of it."

"If we have to make it work, then we shouldn't be doing it. Ross, you promised you wouldn't do this."

"I know, but I can't help it. You are a beautiful woman. I enjoy your company. I'm in love with you, Adriana."

Her eyes turned toward the water as her mother's warning came back to her.

"Ross, I'm sorry. I do love you, but I'm not in love with you. Please tell me you understand."

He rose to his feet and walked to the water's edge. "You're still in love with him aren't you?"

"Who?"

"Come on, surely you're not going to make me spell it out."

Her eyes moistened, "It's complicated."

He turned to look at her, "Of course it is; he's an arse."

"Ross, please don't be like this."

"Why are you defending him? After what he did to you? You deserve better."

Tears began to trickle down her cheeks "Maybe I do, but it's too late to turn back now."

Ross strode over to her and grabbed her hands, "It's not too late. Please Adriana, give us a chance."

She pulled her hands away, "I can't."

"Give me one good reason why not."

A lump caught in her throat. Her mother had been right, she should have told him.

"I'm pregnant, with his child."

Ross's face twisted, "What? ... and you didn't think to tell me?" He turned away from her. "No! Of course not. Let's just string poor gullible Ross along, and let him make a complete fool of himself."

"Ross, please, don't say that. I never meant to hurt you."

He turned to glare at her, "Well, it's a bit damn late for that isn't it?"

He spun on his heel and strode away, "We leave first thing in the morning; be ready."

She got to her feet "Ross, please...wait."

He continued to walk away. Wiping away her tears she sank back  onto the log. As usual she had messed things up. Her head dropped into her hands. A little tap on her shoulder caused her look up. Madison stood looking at her, her bottom lip quivering.

"Why is Ross mad, Mommy?"

Adriana drew her into a hug, "It's nothing for you to worry about, darling. He needs to go back to his store, that's all."

 Madison's face fell, "Are we going home?"

Adriana stroked her hair, "Yes baby. I'm sure Grandma has missed us."

At the mention of her grandmother her face lit up, "I'm going to  tell Grandma about the boat and the fish, and..."

Adriana nodded, "I bet Grandma can't wait to hear all about your holiday."

Madison ran back down to the lake edge and began to pick up her toys. Adriana smiled.

"It's alright Madi, we are not leaving until tomorrow."

She rose to her feet, "How about I help you collect all

your toys? We will put them on the porch all ready for tomorrow."

Adriana glanced out across the water, now a little unsure about having to return. It was going to be hard to see him again, let alone tell him he was going to be a father.

They had dinner early. Afterwards, she bathed Madison and got her ready for bed. There was still no sign of Ross by the time she had finished reading Madison her bed time story and had kissed her goodnight.

"Goodnight sweetheart, I'll see you in the morning."

"Mommy, is Ross scared of the dark?"

Adriana smiled, "No darling. He eats lots of carrots so he can see in the dark."

Madison murmured something that Adriana didn't quite catch. She pulled the  door closed and walked slowly back into the kitchen to clear up the dishes. As the night wore on, she found herself imagining all sorts of terrible things that might have befallen him. Every few minutes she found herself moving to the window to peer out into the darkness. She walked to the front door and switched on the outside light for him. As time wore on, she began to pace the floor. This was all her fault; she should have told him the truth in the beginning. Opening the door she stepped out onto the porch. An eerie silence had settled over the pond. The odd hoot of an owl could be heard in the distance. A silver stream of light glittered across the surface of the pond. She made her way down the steps towards the water's edge, giving a little gasp when her bare feet entered the cold water. Her thoughts suddenly were drawn to Hayden. Coming here was supposed to have helped her get over him. Unfortunately it hadn't worked. Her hand brushed over her slightly rounded abdomen. Ross spoke from the darkness, startling her.

"You look so beautiful in the moonlight."

"Ross! Where have you been? I've been worried sick about you."

"I needed a little time to think, I'm sorry, I shouldn't have laid this all on you... I knew from the beginning that you only wanted friendship. I suppose I thought I could change your mind."

"Ross, you don't have to explain. I am as much to blame as you are. My mother insisted that I should tell you about the baby before we left. I had intended to before now, but I was having such a good time. I suppose I wasn't really ready to face the truth."

He moved toward her, "It doesn't matter. I get it you're in love. Let's just drop the whole subject. The thought of you with him is too..."

"Okay, I won't speak of it again."

They walked together back to the house, "So, are we still leaving in the morning?"

Ross nodded his head, "I think it would be for the best, don't you?"

She nodded, " What time do you think we will head out?"

"About nine should be fine, there's no need to rush."

Her hand moved to his arm, and she felt him tense.

"Thank you Ross. For everything. I am truly sorry that I misled you."

He pulled his arm away, hoping she hadn't noticed his discomfort. "Apology accepted, now I'll say goodnight." "Goodnight Ross," she turned and walked towards her room.

His heart clenched. Things between them would never be quite the same again. Sighing he went into his room and closed the door behind him.

The next morning they were up early. Madison was eager to get home. Adriana wasn't looking forward to explaining that she had decided to delay their homecoming by a couple of days. Ross had already agreed on the slight detour. She had been putting this particular chore off for several months now. "Madi I'm sorry, but we won't be seeing Grandma today."

The smile dropped from Madison's face. "Why?"

"I'm sorry baby, but there is something I have to do before we go home. You'll like it, I promise. We are going to see your cousins. They live near the beach and you will have other children your own age to play with."

Madison's eyes brightened, "Can we build sandcastles?"

Thoughts of their time with Hayden sprung to mind. "Yes baby. You can build sandcastles."

# Chapter Twenty One

As soon as Ross pulled the car into the driveway, the front door of the house flew open. Adriana smiled as her sister ran down the path towards them. She jumped out of the car and was immediately wrapped to her sister's generous bosom.

"It's so good to see you," she held Adriana at arm's length. "You look amazing."

"You wouldn't have said that if you had seen me a few weeks ago."

Ross got out of the car, unable to take his eyes off the two women. The family resemblance was unmistakable. Apart from Katrina being slightly heavier set, they could almost be taken for twins. Adriana signalled for him to come over.

"Thanks to Ross here, I feel like a new woman."

Her sister's eyebrows raised, "Oh! I see."

Adriana blushed, "No, that wasn't what I meant. He took us on holiday. The break did me wonders."

Her sister eyed her suspiciously. Adriana glanced over at him "He's a very good, friend. Ross, this is my sister Katrina. Katrina, Ross."

Ross held out his hand and Katrina shook it. "It's very nice to meet you, Ross."

"Likewise," he replied stiffly. He couldn't help but notice the slight differences in them.

Katrina's eyes were more hazel than green and her lips weren't quite as full as Adriana's. Her complexion was fair, but there was a slight sun kissed look to it, unlike Adriana's pale smooth skin.

"So where did you take this sister of mine to put such a rosy glow on her cheeks?"

"I don't think that glow has anything to do with me."

Adriana shot him a warning glance, waving her hand in his general direction "Don't mind him. I'll explain everything later."

Katrina glanced from one to the other. Adriana reached in, unbuckled Madison and lifted her from her seat, perching her one hip. Katrina's hand shot to her mouth.

"She's got so big and she's gorgeous. Just like her aunty."

Adriana laughed, "Excuse me."

"Okay. I suppose you played some small part in it. I can see a little of Alistair in there, though. We have so much catching up to do. Why don't you all come in and have a drink and something to eat?"

Ross walked to the back of the car and pulled out the two

cases Adriana had packed to keep with her.

"I'm sorry, as nice as that sounds, I have to be getting back, I have a store to run."

"Oh right, well it was very nice meeting you Ross. Maybe I will see you some other time."

"Maybe." He closed the back hatch.

"Katrina, would you mind taking Madi inside for a drink? I'll be along in a minute."

Katrina gave her sister a knowing smile. Adriana placed Madison down on the ground. She clutched shyly at Adriana's skirt, as Katrina held out her hand. .

"Hey, what say you come inside for a nice cold drink and a cookie? You can meet your cousins."

Adriana gave her an encouraging little push forward. Madison, not one for being shy for long, took Katrina's hand. Adriana watched as they headed up the path, Madison was already asking her sister a barrage of questions.

Ross walked around to the driver's door. Adriana followed him. They stood in awkward silence.

"Ross, I don't know how I would have coped without you. I'm sorry for dragging you into all this."

He leant over and gave her a kiss on the cheek, "I had hoped it would turn out a little differently." He opened the door, "Well, I had better be off," he slipped into the driver's seat.

She pushed the door closed. He wound down the window. Her feet shuffled in the loose gravel. "Well, goodbye then, can I come and see you when I get back?"

He looked up at her, his eyes glassy, "We might leave it for a bit. Let things settle."

"Oh right, of course... Well, have a safe trip and thanks again for taking the rest of our things back. Just dump it off at Mom's I've told her to expect it."

"Right, see you then."

"See...you." He started the car and reversed out of the driveway. A lump caught in her throat. It would be hard not to see him, especially  having spent the last two and a half weeks together. She sometimes wished she did feel differently towards him. He was kind and generous. A lot like Alistair in many ways. Reluctantly she made her way toward the house.

Seeing it again bought back a barrage of painful memories. Suddenly she felt very alone. It only seemed like yesterday  she was standing at the front door waving Goodbye, as her husband and son left the house. Alistair had always blown her a kiss before reversing his car out of the driveway. Her shoulders slumped. A simple few words could have saved her all this heartache, but no, she had to insist they go. Rick had been looking forward to the boat trip for weeks. She hated to see the disappointment on his face. Alistair had promised to take him out so many times and had had to cancel, due to work commitments. If he hadn't taken him that day, then it would have been months before he would have had the time. That one decision had cost her and her family dearly.

When she finally plucked up enough courage to

walk up the path and enter the house, she was relieved to see that it no longer resembled the home she had once shared with her husband. It was her sister's home now and Adriana was thankful that none of the belongings that she had shared with her family remained. Katrina's husband Barry met Adriana at the sitting room door. He drew her into a firm hug. "Are you okay?"

Adriana gave him a forced smile, "Yes. To be honest this visit is long overdue."

He released her. His kind hazel eyes travelled her face. "If you need anything, you only need ask."

"Thanks, I should be fine, but I know where to find you if I'm not."

She patted his stomach, "It looks like that sister of mine has been feeding you a little too well."

He gave her a generous smile, "Don't you dare say a word to her, or she'll have me on one of those latest fad diets."

Even with the little weight around his middle, he was still a handsome man. His hair was showing hints of a receding, but his pronounced jaw line gave his face a strong square look. Deep dimples appeared in his cheeks whenever he smiled. It was comforting to know he would be there if she needed him. Katrina and Barry had married the year before her and Alistair had, even though Adriana and Alistair had been seeing each other a lot longer.

Adriana glanced out the window. Madison had already made herself at home and was happily playing out in the backyard with her cousins, oblivious to the fact that this had once been their family home. Adriana heart sank.

The next few days were going to be tough. As much as she hated the thought of dredging up the past, it had to be done. Katrina walked up behind her.

"You look like you could do with a cup of tea."

Adriana gave her a strained smile. "That would be great, thanks."

"Why don't you go and sit out on the veranda and I'll bring it out to you."

"Thanks sis." She walked out the back door and settled herself in one of the chairs overlooking the yard. A few minutes later Katrina appeared, carrying two cups. She handed one to Adriana and placed the other one down on the little table between the chairs as she sat down.

"It's great to see you," She placed her hand on her sister's arm. "I'm glad you decided to come."

Adriana looked across at her, "So am I. Look at Madison. It's as if she has known her cousins all her life."

"She certainly got over her shyness in record time."

Adriana gave a little laugh, "It never takes her very long."

Katrina glanced over at Adriana, "So spill, what's going on with you and this Ross feller?"

Adriana frowned, "Nothing, I told you. He's just a friend."

"Hmm, so who's the father then?"

Adriana sat bolt upright, "What, I'm not," she gave a sigh, "how can you tell?"

Katrina laughed, "I'm your sister, I've had two kids of my own and have seen you through two pregnancies. And you keep putting your hand on your abdomen. That in itself is a sure give away." Katrina patted her stomach, "I also have another one on the way."

"Oh you're kidding."

"No."

"Congratulations. You never said." Katrina smiled,

"Neither did you."

Adriana smiled, "Point taken."

Later that night when the kids were all in bed, they sat down again to talk. Adriana filled her in on her predicament.

"As you see, I'm stuck between doing the right thing and protecting the baby."

"So you don't think there is any future for you and this Hayden feller?"

Adriana shook her head, "How could I ever trust him? Anyway it's obvious he isn't ready for any type of commitment."

"But you are going to tell him, right?"

"I don't know. What if they try and take the baby away, or his mother finds out and disinherits him?"

Katrina rolled her eyes, "Nothings ever simple with you, is it? I get that it's not ideal, but can't you just believe that everything will work out, for the best?"

Adriana glared at her sister, "That's easy for you to say, you have a husband."

Tears welled in her eyes. Katrina placed her hand on her sister's.

"I'm sorry, I didn't mean to sound insensitive. You've been through so much. But I believe he has the right to know."

Adriana's back stiffened, "The right?" Tears began to roll down her cheeks. "He lost that right when he chose to let that other woman eat him alive. Maybe his mother was right, I was just a temporary distraction."

"Oh for goodness sake Adriana, you're always so bloody dramatic. Talk to him. If he wants to be in the baby's life, would that be so bad? You said yourself that he's great with Madi and from what you've told me, I don't think he is going to be in any hurry to tell his mother anything."

"Maybe you're right. I'll think about it."

By the time they headed for bed, Adriana had begun to see things a little clearer. Hayden might want to be in the baby's life. Her eyes closed and she tried to imagine the look on his face when she told him he was about to become a father. His face would break out in a beautiful smile. The soft laughter lines would appear at the corners of his mouth and around his eyes. Her body tensed. But his eyes; they could be cold and calculating. He might have rejected her, but she wasn't going to subject their baby to the same fate.

The next morning when Adriana walked into the kitchen she was struck with a feeling of déjà vu. Katrina was standing against the counter. Her husband's arms were wrapped around her slightly rounded belly as he nibbled on her neck. Adriana let out a startled gasp, and quickly stepped back, coming up against the door frame. Barry turned and saw the look on her face. He dropped his arms and moved toward her. Adriana held up her hand to stop him.

"I'm fine..., honestly."

Katrina turned to look at her, "Are you sure? You've gone very pale."

"Seeing you both there reminded me of Alistair. He used to do the same thing to me."

Deep creases appeared across Barry's forehead, "I'm sorry. We'll try and be a bit more considerate of your feelings."

Adriana gave a strained laugh, "Don't you dare. I can deal with it. This is your home now. I just need a bit of time to adjust, that's all."

Katrina nodded, "Take all the time you need."

Adriana smiled weakly "Thanks Sis."

"Do you want a cup of tea?"

Adriana sat down at the table "Do I ever. By the way, I've been doing some thinking about the house."

Katrina and Barry exchanged worried looks. "I've decided I won't be coming back. I would like to buy a house in Rockland, so I can be near Mom."

Katrina pushed a cup of tea toward her "But you always loved it here. Are you sure?"

"Believe me, I've given it a great deal of thought. There are too many memories here and I want Madison to grow up around her Grandmother. Mom has played a huge part in Madison's life and I wouldn't feel right taking that away from her now."

Katrina shook her head, "And what about Hayden?"

"What about him? It's a big town. I'm sure we can both live there without tripping over each other."

"So have you thought about when you might sell? Barry and I will need time to find somewhere else to live."

"Why?"

"You just said you're selling."

Adriana smiled, "Look, don't worry about it just yet. I'm sure we can come to some sort of arrangement. We'll talk about it later."

She rose to her feet, "I'm heading down to the basement. It's not going to sort itself. I'll take my cup of tea with me."

Katrina studied her sister's face, "Do you want me to come with you?"

"No... I really need to do this on my own. I might need a little help later though, to bring some of it up."

Katrina noted the sadness in her sister's eyes, "Be sure to call me if you need me. In the mean time I'll try and keep Madison occupied."

Adriana walked over and gave her sister a hug "Thanks... for everything."

"What are sisters for? Now go get started before we both start crying. I'll bring you down some refreshments in about an hour, if that's okay."

"That'd be great. Well, here goes" Adriana turned and headed out the door.

Katrina turned to her husband, "Do you think she'll be okay down there all on her own?"

Barry slipped his arm around Katrina's waist. "Don't worry, she'll be fine. She's tough. Look what she's already been through."

"I suppose you're right. I worry about her, and this

Hayden fellow. If I could get my hands on him, I'd show him what happens if you mess with my sister."
Barry smiled, "You're so sexy when you're all fired up."
Her eyes narrowed, "And when I'm not?"
He smiled, drawing her into his arms. "Damn irresistible."
She snuggled against him. "You say the nicest things."

# Chapter Twenty Two

Hayden stormed into the ice cream parlour, his jaw clenched tightly. He strode up to the counter just as Ross appeared from the back room. His cold grey eyes fixed on Ross.

"Where the hell is she?"

"Who?" replied Ross casually, unwilling to allow himself to be  riled.

Hayden's eyes narrowed as he leant over the counter. "You know damn well who. Now where is she?"

Ross smiled smugly, "I think if she had wanted you to know, she would have told you already."

Hayden slammed his fist down on the counter, "I'm not going to ask again."

 Ross stared back at him, "Ask all you want, you certainly won't be getting anything out of me."

Hayden's body tensed, "I'm warning you. Stay the hell away from her."

Ross gave a little cynical laugh, "You've got a bloody nerve, after what you did to her."

Hayden gritted his teeth, "I didn't do anything to her."

"A typical answer from someone like you. Why don't you just leave her alone? You don't deserve her. Go and find yourself a blonde bimbo to amuse yourself with."

Hayden's fists clenched, "You had better watch your mouth."

Ross stepped back from the counter, sensing Hayden was near breaking point.

"She asked me not to tell you and unless she says otherwise, you're shit out of luck."

"I need to see her."

"Why? So you can convince her of what a great guy you are? And that you weren't going at it with some blonde bimbo in your office?"

"That is none of your business."

"If it hurts Adriana, I'll make it my business. She has been through so much already and you are just adding to her problems!"

Hayden leant over the counter and grabbed the collar of Ross's shirt. He pulled his face close.

"I won't lose her. Not to the likes of you."

"You've already blown any chance you had with her. The sooner you realise that, the better."

Hayden released him, shoving him backwards. He turned to leave.

"Tell her I need to see her."

"I'll tell her nothing of the sort."

With one swift movement Hayden swiped everything off the counter.

"I'm not asking. I will see her, one way or another."

He stalked out of the store, slamming the door behind him. Ross turned to the young girl standing behind him. "Did you see that? What a bastard. I don't know what Adriana ever saw in him."

The young girl nodded her eye's still locked on the door. "Ah...huh."

Ross groaned, "Not you too? Have all females gone completely mad?" He stormed off into the back room.


Katrina made her way down the stairs. Adriana was sitting amongst a pile of opened boxes, smiling down at the photograph in her hand. She glanced up as her sister approached.

"I didn't realize how much I had kept. In the last hour, I have laughed and cried so much, my  sides hurt."

 Katrina placed a plate with two scones on it and a glass of apple juice down on the boxes beside her, "I thought you might be ready for a break."

Adriana smiled "I am, thanks. I have actually managed to sort through quite a lot. I'm giving all that to charity," she said waving her hand towards a pile of boxes stacked haphazardly over in the corner of the room.

Katrina glanced over, "Are you sure? You don't need to make a decision right now."

"Too late. The decision's been made. It's all going tomorrow."

"If you're sure, I'll have Barry take it out in the morning. Out of your way."

Adriana nodded, "That would be  great. Preferably before I change my mind." She glanced down at the picture clasped firmly in her hand, placing it in the pile next to her. Tears began to trickle down her cheeks. Katrina sat down beside her and slipped her arm around her sister's shoulder. "I knew this was going to be hard, I just never realised how hard."

Katrina pulled her closer, "If I could take all this hurt away I would. You know that, don't you?"

Adriana turned her tear stained face to look at her sister, "I know. Thanks for being here... Now go, I've got work to do."

Katrina got to her feet. Bending down she kissed the top of her sister's head. "I know when I'm not wanted. Eat your scones. And I'm warning you now, you are stopping for lunch. No excuses.  The baby  will be hungry by then."

Adriana smiled, "Go."

She  let out a small sigh as she looked at the pile in front of her. This was what her past amounted to. A pile of painful memories. She picked up the next box and began to sort through it.


A couple of hours later, she was sitting on the back porch with everyone else, eating  lunch. She placed her empty  plate  down  on the table and leant back in the chair.

"I think I ate too much. I must be making up for all those weeks I hardly ate anything."

Katrina looked across at her, "Has your morning sickness gone?

Adriana shook her head, "It's not as bad as it was. It usually occurs first thing in the morning. After about an hour it seems to come right."

"How are you doing downstairs?"

"Not bad. It's going to take me a while. I still have to get everything I want to keep to Mom's yet. I can't very well take it all back on the bus."

"You don't have to worry about that. Barry and I can see to it. We've been thinking that maybe it would be a good idea to drive you back. We could make a long weekend of it."

"I don't want to put you out."

"Oh for goodness sake Adriana. It wouldn't be putting us out. We've been meaning to get up and see Mom. If we don't go now" she patted her stomach. "Who knows when we will be able to manage it?"

Adriana smiled, "Mom will be thrilled to see you all. She keeps talking about coming down, but never seems to get around to it."

"Tell me about it. I've been asking her for months."

"Don't worry it's nothing personal, she was the same when I was living down here."


Later that day Adriana went out onto the balcony alone. Her eyes moistened as she looked out over the ocean. They had built this house together. The view had been one of the things she had loved  most about the house. Now, it just made her sad. She blinked back tears, remembering back to the day she had watched her husband and son sail out to sea. For days afterwards she had sat in this very spot, praying for their safe return. Wiping away the tears she entered the house. Barry and Katrina were sitting on the sofa.

"You can have it."

Katrina looked up from what she was doing. "Have what?"

"The house."

"Adriana, don't be so foolish. You love this house"

"I used to love it. I don't anymore."

"Adriana, surely you can't mean to give it away. Why don't you leave it a while longer, and then see how you feel?"

"I don't want it. I could never live here again, but I would feel much better knowing that you are here. Alistair loved this house. We both did. I wouldn't want some stranger living in it."

"I won't simply take it from you Adriana, you need the money to secure your future."

"What if you bought it then?"

"I'm not sure we could afford it, with another baby on the way. It would be well above our price range."

Adriana looked across at her sister, "Why don't you go to the bank and at least see what they would be willing to lend you? Whatever it is, we'll make the asking price."

"I couldn't; you need the money just as much as we do."

"I'm managing, and even if you can only borrow half of what this is worth it will see me right. Now that's the end of it. Make the appointment see what your bank manager is willing to loan you, then we will go from there."

Katrina glanced across at Barry, could they really own this beautiful house with it spectacular ocean views? A house which over the past two years had become their home?

The next day Katrina and Barry headed down to the bank. The loan they were offered came to about two thirds of the property value. That very same day Adriana signed the house over to them. As her pen left the paper, she felt a huge weight lift off her shoulders. Finally she was free. It had once been their dream home. They had designed it together, right down to the brass window catches. Everything about the house reminded her of their life together. If she kept it, it would only make it harder for her to move on. Adriana got up from  the chair and walked out onto the balcony. The house was no longer hers. Tears slid down her cheeks. Katrina slipped her arm around her sister's shoulder.

"Thank you, sis. This means so much to us."

Adriana forced a smile, "It means a great deal more to me, knowing that the house is in safe hands. As long as I'm welcome to visit."

"Our house is your house, you are welcome any time."

# Chapter Twenty Three

Barry blasted the car horn. "Barry, please have a little patience. She's saying goodbye."

"Sorry, but we need to get going. The kids are getting grumpy."

Adriana walked through the house one last time. Tears rolled down her cheeks as she stood in the doorway of the master bedroom. Their two children had been conceived in this room. She placed her hand on her belly. This was to be a new chapter in her life. Reluctantly she turned and made her way down the stairs, her fingers trailed along the hand carved banister. They had argued over which one they were going to get. Alistair had finally given in and let her have her way. As she stepped out onto the front porch, she turned to take one last look down the hall,  then pulled the  door  closed. She slid into the  seat beside

Madison.

"Let's go and see Grandma."

Barry started the car and reversed out of the driveway. Steeling herself against the sudden well of emotion, she forced herself not to look back. From now on she would focus on the future, no matter what it held. Her thoughts drifted to Hayden. Her mother had passed on his messages, but she had chosen to ignore them. It was hard to know what to feel. The word 'betrayed' came to mind. Would he already be lavishing his attention on some other woman? She glanced out of the window, blinking back tears. It had all been a stupid mistake. How could she have let herself fall in love with a man like him? In a way she felt sorry for him. It was hard to imagine what it would be like to go through life with a mother like that. One who dictated who you could and couldn't see, and who you should marry. If that had been her, she would have told her mother where she could stick her money. Living under someone's thumb like that wasn't something she could accept.

As they pulled into the driveway, a smile touched on Adriana's lips. It felt so good to be home at last. Madi was already struggling to get out of her seat before the car had even stopped. Adriana gave an exasperated sigh.

"Will you please sit still so I can unbuckle you?"

"There's Grandma" Madison cried, waving her little hand frantically through the window.

Finally Adriana managed to release the buckle. Madison scrambled across her knee and out of the open door. By the time Adriana got out of the car, Madison was already in her  grandmother's arms.

"Goodness me Madi, you've got so big. I won't be able to pick you up soon."

Adriana smiled as she walked up the steps, "Hi Mom, it's so good to be home. I've missed you."

"I've missed you both terribly. The house has been so quiet without you."

At that moment a tall, handsome grey haired man appeared in the doorway. Adriana's brow furrowed.

"Oh, sorry, this is Brian. Brian, this is my daughter Adriana and my granddaughter Madison."

Adriana looked at her mother questioningly, "Had a little something to fill the void, have we?"

Her mother cheeks flushed. Brian held out his hand and Adriana shook it.

"It's nice to meet you Brian."

He nodded, "Likewise. I've heard so much about you all. It's  good to finally put faces to the names."

Adriana's eyes caught her mother's. "I wish I could say the same, but I'm afraid my mother has kept you a secret."

Brian draped his arm casually across her mother's shoulder, "Knowing your mother, I'm sure she had her reasons."

Katrina and Barry came up the steps behind Adriana, and so began the barrage of kissing and hugging as the family reacquainted themselves with each other. Finally, they all moved inside. The luggage was dropped at the door to be sorted later. All the children quickly disappeared out the back to play. A look passed between Adriana and Katrina, as their mother sat down on the chair and Brian perched himself on the arm beside her, taking her hand in his.

"So Mom, I have to ask, how long has this been going on?" Adriana asked, waving her hand in their general direction.

Her mother smiled and looked up at him with nothing but pure devotion. "Eleven months, twelve days, six hours..."

"Okay I get it. So why the secrecy?"

"I couldn't bring myself to tell you. Not with everything you were going through. You were having such a rough time of it all."

"Oh Mom, you don't need to protect me. I'm a grown woman, I would have coped."

Adriana looked over at Brian and approved of what she saw. She guessed him to be in his mid fifties. He was well dressed and had a casual friendly manner that put her at ease immediately. He noticed her looking at him and gave her a warm smile, his bright blue eyes studying her intently, as though asking for her approval.

She smiled, "Well Brian, welcome to our family," She looked over at her mother. "Hopefully, we will have plenty of opportunities to get to know you, since you already seem to know a lot about us."

He smiled, "I'm sure you will."


Later that night the three women sat together out in the garden. Barry and Brian were in the kitchen bonding over the dishes which they had insisted on doing. "You know Mom, you could have told me about him.

I wouldn't have been upset. I like him and it's obvious he likes you too."

"I was going to tell you, but then that thing happened with you and Hayden and suddenly you were telling me you were pregnant and going away with Ross."

Adriana took her mother's hand in hers "I'm sorry about all that, but I needed a bit of time to get my head straight."

Her mother's eyes met hers "And with all this free time, did you come to a decision about what you're going to do?"

Katrina spoke up "Mom, talk to her. I've tried to convince her that she needs to go and see him and at the very least tell him about the baby."

Adriana turned and glared at her sister, "I will. It's just that I'm scared of what his reaction will be."

Her mother smiled, "You know, you might be pleasantly surprised. He's been asking after you almost every day. I was almost expecting him to be waiting here for you, when you arrived."

"I heard he even paid Ross a little visit and wasn't too happy when Ross wouldn't tell him where you were."

Adriana gasped, "He went to see Ross? Why? How did he know?" Tears welled in her eyes, "What a mess I've created."

"Well, I did try and warn you."

"I know, and I should have listened to you. Poor Ross." She could see Hayden storming into the store temper flaring, his cold grey eyes fixed on Ross. Ross had been such a good friend to her, he didn't deserve to be on the receiving end of Hayden's wrath.  Maybe she should go down and apologise but how could she? Hadn't she promised him she would stay away?

The rest of the family had long since gone to bed. Adriana lay on her bed staring up at the ceiling. Her life was going to change, whether  she wanted it to or not. In approximately six months time she would be holding her new born baby in her arms. She wished she had some insight as to how he was going to receive the news that she was pregnant, with his child. Time was running out. The doctor had been right; the longer you left it the harder it became. Her eyes glistened. She certainly didn't want him hearing it from someone else, but she wasn't sure if she was strong enough to see him again just yet. It still hurt to think of his betrayal. Ahead of her lay some very big decisions. For a start there was the store to consider. It was going to be difficult to run a business and raise a baby, even with her mother's help. It would be unfair of her to lay this burden on her mother, when there was a new man in her life now. Adriana couldn't bring herself to jeopardize her mother's happiness by putting unnecessary demands on her. She sighed. It would be a shame to sell the store after all her hard work. But if she had to choose between the store or her children, then the store would have to go.

# Chapter Twenty Four

Four weeks had passed since her return, and she still hadn't found the courage to confront him. Barry and Katrina had returned home, leaving Adriana to ponder her predicament. Hayden had phoned several times since she had been back, but she had refused to talk to him. What she had to tell him she knew would have to be done face to face. She gave a little sigh. For the past couple of weeks now the phone had remained silent. Had he finally given up on her? Did he have one of his prepared' let down speeches' ready for her? Was he now seeing someone else? A lump caught in her throat as she slipped quietly out onto the back porch. Dropping down in one of the chairs, she rested her head back and closed her eyes. A dull throb pounded against her temples. The back door opened and closed. Forcing her eyes open, she blinked against the bright sunlight.

Brian stood above her. "Mind if I join you, or would you rather be alone?"

She gave him a weak smile, "Be my guest. Being alone isn't all it's cracked up to be."

"Your mother told me about your situation."

"I thought she might."

"Do you mind if I give you a little advice, from a male's perspective?"

She gave a little wave of her hand, "Go ahead. Everyone else has."

"They only care about you."

Adriana looked across at him, "I know, I'm sorry. I didn't mean to sound ungrateful, you have all been really great. I wish this would all just go away." Her hand flew to her mouth, "Oh... not the baby, I didn't mean...."

He reached over and patted her hand, "I know what you meant."

Silence hung between them, "So what's the advice?"

"It's not really advice, it's more like questions."

A deep crease crept across her brow, "I'm not sure I like the sound of that."

"Don't worry, they are just simple question, but the answers might help you shed some light on your troubles."

"I'm listening."

"Firstly... do you love him?"

Her eyes moistened, "I.. I don't see what that has to do with it."

"A simple yes or no is all I ask."

She wiped her eyes "Okay..., as much as it pains me to say it, yes... I love him."

"Do you think he at least deserves the chance to explain?"

"No..."

Brian's eyebrows rose.

"Fine... yes, I suppose he does."

"Do you think he would purposely want to hurt you or Madison?"

She thought back to the time he had taken her out on the boat to say goodbye to her lost family, "No... he wouldn't."

"Do you think he would be a good father?"

Her finger's tightened on the chair, "Yes, damn it."

"And finally, do you think he should know he's about to become a father?"

"Okay, okay... I get it."

He smiled, "See, I told you it was simple. Now go and see him."

"How did you get to be so wise about matters of the heart?"

He grinned, "That's my little secret. Now go."


Adriana walked into the kitchen and gave her mom a hug. "Brian's great. I think you have a keeper there."

"I've already worked that one out for myself, but thank you anyway."

"I'm just going out for a bit to get some fresh air. I'll be back for dinner."

Her mother tilted her head to the side and smiled, "You're

going to see him, aren't you?"
Adriana eyes narrowed "Have you two been plotting together?"
"No, of course not."
"Mother!"
"Fine, we have. But we did it for your own good. You've been moping around here for weeks now."
"I know. I'm sorry I've been such a pain."
Her mother wrapped her arms around her, "I can understand the hesitation, but this won't go away by itself."
"I know.  Brian just gave me the push I needed."
She turned to leave, "Wish me luck."
"I would, but  honestly I don't think you will need it."
Adriana's eyes widened, "Do you know something I don't?"
"Call it women's intuition."
"Well, I hope you're right."
Adriana pulled her coat from the hook behind the door and glanced back at her mother, giving her a forced grin.
"I feel like I'm walking into a lion's den."
"You'll be fine. It's never as bad as you imagine it to be."
"I hope you're right," Adriana replied, as she pulled the door closed behind her.

As she marched down the road with a renewed determination, her hand instinctively moved to her abdomen. "I'll sort this, don't worry," she said, more to herself than the baby. When she reached the street that led out to the bay, her pace slowed. She still wasn't quite sure what seeing him again would do to her. At nights she still ached to be held by him and his face haunted her dreams. Reaching the bay, she stopped for a minute to breath in the fresh sea air. Her eyes were instinctively drawn out to sea, And her body gave a little shiver as she pulled her coat tighter around her expanding frame. Time had passed so quickly, it was hard to believe it was already heading into the fall. Soon snow would be appearing on the mountain peaks behind her. The beaches would again be deserted and the trees bare.

Reluctantly she pushed on, making her way along the beach, trying to convince herself she was doing the right thing. Her heart wrenched when she moved past the spot where they had first been together. She could still remember the intense feelings which had engulfed her. Had she actually fallen in love with him at that very moment? Her hand gently stroked her stomach; she gave a forced laugh, and "you were conceived on this very spot."
When she finally reached the path that led up to his house she hesitated. What if he wasn't home, what if he demanded she leave? She took a deep breath. "It's never as bad as it seems." She muttered to herself. The shells crunched noisily beneath her feet as she slowly made her way up the path. Drawing to a stop, she stood under a canopy of trees looking up at the house. The doors to the upstairs balcony stood wide open, a sure sign that he was home. Taking a couple of tentative steps forward she suddenly froze. Voices drifted down from the opened

doorway. Her body stiffened, as the familiarity of Hayden's voice engulfed her. A soft feminine giggle soon followed. Two figures appeared on the balcony above. She stepped back out of sight as fresh tears sprung to her eyes. The woman draped her arm across his shoulder and kissed his cheek. He turned and grabbed her in a fierce hug. A playful squeal floated down from above. Unable to watch any longer, Adriana turned and fled back down the path, quickly making her way along the beach. Gasping for breath she finally reached the shoreline. Sinking down on one of the rocks, she fought to regain her breath. She swiped irritably at the tears now coursing down her cheeks.

Hayden and his sister stood in the doorway leading out to the balcony, "So what are  you going to do?"

His brow creased, "Do?"

"About Adriana."

"Why should I do anything?"

Janice walked over to the railing and stood looking out over the bay, "Because it's making you miserable."

"It was her choice. I've tried contacting her. She won't answer my calls."

Her eye brows rose, "Since when has that stopped you?"

"What's the point? It's over."

She gave a little laugh, "You keep telling yourself that, and one day you might actually believe it."

"Come on, Janice. She went off with another man, doesn't that say it all?"

"Oh Hayden, don't you know anything about women?"

"Of course I do. I'm not a complete idiot."

"So tell me, why didn't she just say that she didn't want to see you anymore? Why all the drama? It would have been a lot easier."

He turned to glare at her, "So, Miss 'know it all'. Why won't she take my calls?"

She gave an exasperated sigh, "Think about it from her point of view. She's been through so much all ready. You were the first man she had let into her life since losing her husband and son. For goodness sake Hayden, she saw you with another woman. What was she supposed to think? Can't you see? She's protecting herself and her child? Besides, didn't the guy she went away with, come back alone?"

He walked over to the railing ""Yes... so you think there is still a chance that she feels something for me?"

"Duh... of course I do."

"Oh, and you're sure of that are you?"

She smiled "More than sure. I saw the way she looked at you."

He sighed. He missed those beautiful green eyes looking at him like he was the only thing in the world that mattered. His eyes scanned the bay, as they did every day hoping to catch sight of her. His body suddenly stiffened as his eyes were drawn to a solitary figure sitting on the rocks by the shore line. The glass he was holding slipped from his grasp and fell to the floor.

"Hayden, what an earth...?" she followed his gaze.

"Is that her?"

"I don't know, but I'm sure as hell going to find out." He leapt over the balcony railing and landed on the ground below, rolling forward on his shoulder then flipping over onto his feet. Janice smiled as he cursed loudly, knowing better than to ask if he was okay. He was fit and agile and it would take more than a clumsy landing to stop him. She watched him sprint down the path and onto the beach favouring one leg  slightly. Out of all her siblings he was the one she felt deserved happiness the most. It seemed to have eluded him up until  now. He was in love with her, that was obvious. Her hand went up to shield her eyes from the sun as she watched him approaching the figure. He had now slowed to a walk.

"Adriana" he called softly as he drew closer. Her breath caught in her throat, but she was too scared to turn around. He moved closer and let out a relieved sigh when he saw it was her. Words seemed to fail him. He had waited so long for this moment. Now it was here, he didn't know what to say to her. He jumped when she spoke.

"Hi Hayden."

"Adriana,"

 She glanced up at him. He could see she had been crying. He wanted more than anything to wrap her in his arms and comfort her. Jealousy was a funny thing and often had you acting in ways that were totally  irrational.

"When did you get back?"

She sniffed, "Four weeks ago."

"Four weeks..! Why didn't you contact me?  I left enough

messages”

“I needed time to sort a few things out.”

His body tensed, “Time!” He ran his fingers through his hair. “Well, that’s just great... so are you all sorted now?”

Her eyes narrowed, “As a matter of fact, I am. It was stupid of me to come here.”

“What! You sit out here knowing there is a chance I might see you. When I do come down here you offer no explanation, and now you say you shouldn’t have come. So why did you bother?”

She shrugged her shoulders.

He gave an exasperated sigh, “That’s not an answer.”

She wiped at her eyes, “I did want to see you. Until I saw you on the balcony with one of your latest conquests. I realised I had made a huge mistake coming back here.”

A frown creased his brow, “What the hell are you talking about?”

“Oh please, don’t act all innocent with me. I’m not blind. You were with a woman., on the balcony.”

His fists clenched, “I don’t think you have the right to be pointing the finger. Didn’t you go off with that guy Ross?”

Her eyes narrowed, “He’s a friend.”

“So you say. So let me get this right. It’s alright for you to go off with another man, but I can’t have woman friends, is that it?”

She shot to her feet, “My friends don’t feel inclined to give me lap dances.”

His body tensed. She had seen it. “Jessica is not a friend.”

Adriana gave him a 'told you so' look. "That was plainly obvious. Your hands were all over her."

His jaw tensed, "She finds it hard to take no for an answer. And for your information, my hands weren't all over her. I was holding her away."

Her eyes narrowed, "Sure.. that's exactly what it looked like," she replied sarcastically.

"My mother put her up to it. She saw your name in the appointment book and arranged for Jessica to be there when you turned up."

A knot formed in Adriana's stomach as she recalled the conversation she had had with his mother in the lift, and the smug look on Jessica's face.

"Your mother's a right royal bitch."

He smiled, "I would have to agree."

"She warned me off."

He frowned. "What? Warned you off how? When?"

She sighed, "The day I came to the office and saw you..., with that woman. Your mother caught me in the elevator on the way out and informed me that you would lose your inheritance if I continued to see you."

He stood staring at her open mouthed, "She did, huh? Well doesn't that just top it all? And you believed her. You didn't think to check with me first, before running off with the first available man?"

"Of course I believed her, and you were otherwise occupied.... So, you're saying she lied?"

He let out a deep throaty laugh, "Yes that's exactly what I'm saying. My mother only owns ten percent of the shares in the company; the rest are split equally between me, my two brothers and three sisters. One of whom, I'm sure wouldn't appreciate being called my latest conquest."

Tears welled in her eyes. He took her hands in his and drew her against him. Her hand came up between them as she pushed away from him.

"I can't."

He frowned " Adriana please, it's all been a big misunderstanding. I've missed you."

She turned her tear stained face up to his, "There's something else you need to know."

His jaw tightened, "If you are about to say there is another man in your life, don't. I'll kill him."

Adriana blinked back her tears, "I'm pregnant."

He gasped stepping away from her.

Her eyes glistened as she stared up at him.

Suddenly his eyes turned cold, "Is it..." he couldn't bring himself to ask.

Her hands went to her hips, "Is it, what? Yours? Is that what you were going to ask? You know what... I am not even going to dignify that with an answer." She drew her coat tighter around her body and turned to leave.

He grabbed her arm "Adriana! I need to know."

"Why? So you can have a clear conscience and sleep at night." She said snatching her arm away as she tried to push past him.

He stepped out to block her way.

"Get out of my way!" she screamed.

He stood his ground. A fresh flood of tears began to stream down her face, "Please..., Hayden..., just let me past."

His eyes softened, "Adriana, tell me. Is the baby mine?"
She looked up at him, her lashes wet with tears. "Of course it's yours! I'm four months pregnant, you do the maths."
His mouth dropped open but no words were spoken.
"Well, aren't you going to say anything?"
"I thought Ross was..., oh to hell with what I thought." He moved towards her, pulling her against him. Still angry she tried to push him away.
"Please, Adriana, forgive me. I'm an idiot. I need you in my life. You have just made me the happiest man in the world."
Her eyes widened, "Happy?... but I thought..."
He gazed down at her, his eyes soft with tears. "We both think far too much. I want nothing more than us to be a family. These past weeks, I have been miserable without you."
She looked up at him, stunned beyond belief. His response was more than she had dared hope for. Suddenly the world went black and she went limp in his arms.

When she awoke she was lying on his sofa, the face of a woman she didn't recognize, looking down on her worriedly.
"Hi... you're back. Don't worry. I'm Janice, Hayden's sister. Not the ideal circumstances to meet in, I know. But I am glad to meet you finally."
Adriana's face flushed as she recalled what she had said about her. "Where's Hayden?" she asked, still feeling a little disorientated.

"Oh, he'll be along in a minute. He's just gone to fetch you a glass of water."

A few seconds later a worried Hayden returned to the room. His sister moved off the couch and Hayden sat down beside her.

"What happened?"

He smiled "I told you I wanted us to be a family and you went and fainted on me. Gave me a heck of a scare."

Adriana lay staring up at him, a blank look on her face.

His brows drew together. "We can be a family, can't we?"

Adriana smiled, "If you're sure you are up to it. I can't have you walking out when the first dirty nappy needs changing."

"I've had to endure years with my mother. That should prepare me for anything. I promise you, I'm not going anywhere."

She reached for his hand and placed it on her belly, "Can you feel the baby kicking?"

Hayden nodded, a triumphant grin spreading across his face.

"A boy for sure with a kick like that."

"And if it's a girl? How will you handle living with a houseful of females?"

His eyes sought hers, "I'll have them falling at my feet."

She gave him a playful slap. He lowered his lips to hers and she felt the all too familiar desire race through her body. He finally forced himself to pull away.

"I've missed you so much."

Her eyelashes fluttered, "Not as much as I ha..." she patted her stomach, "we have."

He grinned "By the way. I did the maths. Was the baby conceived on the beach?"

She nodded, flushing. "I didn't think you wanted to be a father."

"That was before you and Madi came into my life. You could have a football team and I'd still be the happiest man alive."

"Well, I don't think we will be creating any football teams. But we could practice. You have a little catching up to do."

He gave her a sly grin, "My thoughts exactly." He suddenly stiffened, "What about the baby... Is it all right to....?"

Adriana laughed, "I assure you, the baby won't mind a bit."

"I'll be gentle I promise."

She gave him a disappointed look, "Not too gentle I hope. You can't hurt the baby, you know."

"Oh right... I knew that."

Janice walked to the door "I think that's my cue to leave."

A flush appeared on Adriana's cheeks, "I'm sorry... I forgot you...."

"Think no more about it. I'm just glad to see him smiling again. Enjoy your time together, and congratulations to the both of you. I'll catch up with you later. Oh and Hayden, keep a hold of her this time. You do that and I'll make sure Mother stays out of your way."

He smiled, "Deal. Don't worry, I'm not about to let her

out of my sight any time soon."

"Thanks," called Adriana from the couch.

"Yeah, thanks Sis. For everything. Now I don't mean to be rude, but can you get the hell out of here?"

Adriana blushed, "Hayden!"

"Don't worry, she gets it."

"Gets what, exactly?"

"That her brother is in love."

Adriana smiled, "Is he just. Well, maybe he should shut his mouth and show his woman just how much he loves her."

He groaned as he lifted her off the couch "You have got a little heavier." He pretended to struggle as he carried her up the stairs and into the bedroom. He laid her on the bed.

She laughed, "What? No sand dunes?"

He grinned, "There will be plenty of time for sand dunes believe me."

He dropped down on to the bed beside her. Her deep green eyes looked up at him. His heart began to pound in his chest. He laid his hand on her rounded belly and closed his eyes. It was hard to believe that he now had his very own family. One who would never feel the pain of rejection. Or ever be ignored. They would know what it was like to be loved unconditionally. His thoughts drifted to Madison. He had missed her cute little ways. Now she was going to be a part of his family.

"What are you smiling about?"

He gazed down at her. How was it possible to love someone as much as he loved her? "I was thinking of Madi actually, and how much I've missed her."

Adriana smiled, "I think the feeling's mutual."
"I will be a good father to her, I promise."
"I already know that. Now stop grinning at me like some love struck schoolboy and make love to me. I'm going crazy here."
"Oh, right" he lowered his lips to hers as her body quivered with wanting.

# Chapter Twenty Five

Adriana clutched Hayden's hand, determined not to scream as another contraction tore though her body. All she wanted was for it to be over. Everyone had told her that being her third child, things would be easier. She was yet to see it. At five hours she had already surpassed the length of Madison's entire labour. As the time passed, Hayden seemed to become more and more agitated. He found it hard to believe that women would put themselves through this, time and time again, knowing what it would do to them. The doctor smiled, good news.

You should be ready to push on this next one."

Adriana dropped her head back down on the pillow, "About time."

As the next contraction set in she let out a small groan and bore down.

"Okay, Adriana that's great. A few more like that and you'll soon be holding your baby in your arms."

Hayden glanced up at the clock. Twenty minutes had passed since she began pushing. Surely it couldn't be much longer? Adriana squeezed his hand.
"Are you okay?"
He gave her a reassuring smile, "Sure but can we speed this up?"
 Her body tensed as she bore down again. The doctor looked up at her.
"The baby's head is crowning. One more good push when you're ready." She bore down. "Perfect. Give me a second here. Okay, here we go. This should be the last one."
With good push, she felt the baby slip from her body. Her breath caught in her chest as she waited for the reassuring sound of the baby's cry. Her hand gripped Hayden's tightly as her eyes focused on the doctor. A loud wail filled the room. Relief washed over her as she dropped her head back down on the pillow. A broad grin spread across Hayden's face.
"It's a boy. Adriana, we have a son." His eyes moistened as he leant over and kissed her cheek, Thank you."
The doctor cleared his throat, "Hayden,  would you like to cut the cord?"
Hayden moved to the end of the bed, a little hesitantly. His hands were shaking as he took the scissors from the nurse. The doctor smiled.
"Don't look so worried, you can't hurt him."
Hayden snipped the cord and watched as the doctor tied it

off. He looked up at Adriana, a proud grin on his pale face. The nurse took the baby to quickly check him over and clean him up a little. She returned minutes later with him wrapped snugly in a blanket and handed him to Adriana. She looked down at their perfect little son. He had a faint covering of blonde hair over the top of his head.

Hayden sat down on the edge of the bed to admire him. His eyes were wet. "Adriana, you have just made me the happiest man in the world."
She laughed, "There are probably hundreds of men around the world saying the exact same thing at this very moment."
"I guess so," he smiled, "being a father is the most amazing feeling. We produced a complete new little person."
Adriana smiled up at him, "We did didn't we? Now if you can possibly stand a minute apart from us, could you go out into the waiting area and tell everyone that you now have a son? And while you're out there, bring Madi in, so she can meet her new baby brother."
The doctor glanced up at Hayden as he left, "Take your time, and give us a chance to finish up in here. Hayden nodded, then left though rather reluctantly.

As he entered the waiting room, his sister rushed over to him.
"Adriana and the baby are fine. It was touch and go for me though. I nearly couldn't stomach it. I don't know

how women go through that time and time again."

"So, come on... do you have a son or a daughter?"

A broad grin spread across his face, "We have a son."

Madi came running across the room, throwing herself at Hayden. He grabbed hold of her and lifted her into his arms. "How would you like to come and meet your baby brother?"

She gave delighted squeal, "Yes please. Suddenly, the smile dropped from her face, "Is he ugly?"

Hayden laughed, "No, of course not."

"My friend's baby sister was all wrinkly and pink. She was yucky."

Everyone laughed. Hayden kissed her forehead "Babies can sometimes look a little odd when they're new. You have to remember they have been stuck in Mommy's tummy for nine months, and their skin can sometimes look funny for a little while. Like when you go swimming and stay in the water too long."

"I hope he's not ugly."

Hayden laughed, "I'm sure you'll like him."

He turned to the others in the room, "We can all go through, we just give it about ten minutes or so." He held his hand out to Patricia. "I can't wait for you all to see him."

Janice hugged her brother, "Congratulations Daddy."


Adriana sat propped up against the pillows, the baby was resting on her chest. She looked exhausted but felt extremely happy. The door opened and Madison rushed over to the bed and clambered up beside her mother. She instantly shrank back, "Eeew! He's all wrinkly."

Adriana laughed, "So were you when you were this little."

Madison looked up at her mother in disbelief, "No I wasn't," she replied, sliding off the bed.

Adriana smiled. Patricia walked over and gave her daughter a hug.

"Congratulations, Baby," Tears trickled down her cheeks.

Adriana looks up at her mother, "oh Mom, I'm so happy. I have a son, another chance."

Her mother nodded. Adriana glanced past her mother to the door. "Where's Brian? He should be here."

Her mother smiled, "He will be. He just had to stop off and pick something up on the way." She leant over to look at the baby, "May I hold him?"

"Of course you can." Adriana placed the baby in her mother's arms. Madison took the opportunity to climb up on the bed beside her mother. Adriana put her arm around her daughter and drew her close. Madison snuggled up against her, enjoying being there without the ugly baby near.

"I like my puppy better."

Adriana's brow creased. "Puppy? we don't have a puppy." she said looking up at Hayden.

"Yes we do." said Madi indignantly.

"We do?"

Hayden gave her a sly grin.

"But I've told you we can't have a puppy until we move out of Mom's"

"Don't worry yourself over it; we have it sorted."

"What sorted?"

"Okay. I was going to keep it as a surprise, but since Madi has let the cat or dog out of the bag, I may as well tell you. Both you and Madi are all moved in. I know you said you wanted to wait until after the baby was born, but I thought I would take it upon myself to do it for you."

"But what about your house? It's not exactly Madi proof, and we are yet to sort out a room for the baby."

He grinned, "You worry too much, trust me."

"I do but....."

"No buts, trust me."

"I warned you, she doesn't like surprises."

Hayden slipped his arm around his mother-in-law's shoulder, "Thanks, but I can handle it. You had to put up with a lot in the beginning, but I think you believed deep down, that Adriana and I belonged together. You now get to relax a little, and enjoy the time with that new man of yours" He kissed her on the cheek, "Thanks Mom."

Her eyes widened. He grinned.

"I told you I'd eventually get used to the idea of calling you Mom."

"It took you long enough."

The baby made a soft gurgling sound.

"So, have you decided on a name yet?"

"Tyler Jonathan Radcliff," Hayden said proudly.

Patricia smiled, as she gently stroked the baby's head "Well hello there Tyler, I'm your Grandma. You and I are going to have some great times together."

She glanced up at Adriana, "By the way, your sister says

congratulations and they will come up as soon as they can. The doctor says she shouldn't travel at the moment,  due to her high blood pressure. Katrina said to tell you that once her baby is born, nothing will keep her away."

Adriana's brow creased, "She's okay though, isn't she?"

"She's fine. She only has a few more weeks to go. It would be too stressful for her to try and get all the family up here."

"It'll be so good having babies of a similar age. We can compare notes."

Janice walked over to Patricia, "Can I please have a hold of my nephew?"

"Oh sorry, I was so taken with him, I forgot about everyone else."

Patricia handed him over to Janice, who began to coo and play with Tyler's hands. Adriana and Hayden glanced at each other. "I think someone is getting a little clucky."

Janice looked up and smiled, "Who me? No. I'm not ready for babies just yet. If it's okay with you I'll just come and borrow yours from time to time."

"We might need the services of a good baby sitter."

"I don't know about that. I don't know the first thing about babies."

"You never do. You just learn as you go along."

"You have a bit of time after all, you still haven't found Mr Right yet."

"True." She turned to look at her brother, "but there is hope for me yet. Look at you two. Hayden always swore he wasn't the settling down type. You had only known Adriana for a matter of hours before you got her pregnant."

Adriana gasped, "Janice, there are  young ears in the room."

"Sorry... I forgot."

Hayden turned and glared at his sister. "You sounded just like mother."

Janice's hand flew to her mouth, "Oh my god, I'm turning into my mother, I'm so sorry, both of you."

At that moment the door was abruptly shoved open.


April stood framed in the doorway, her arms folded across her chest and her mouth set in a firm line.

"So why wasn't I told?"

"Speak of the devil" muttered Janice under her breath.

Hayden stepped in front of her, "Mother, I'm not having a scene... Not here. I think it might be best if you left."

"I will do no such thing. I have every right to see my grandchild."

Adriana saw Hayden's body tense. "Hayden, it's fine really. Let your mother see her grandson."

Hayden shot her a worried glance. Adriana smiled reassuringly at him. April gave a triumphant humph and walked over to Janice and held out her arms. Janice reluctantly placed Tyler in them. Hayden gasped as a smile broke out across his mother's face.

"He looks a little like you, my boy," she said glancing up at her son proudly."

Hayden's mouth dropped open. He glanced back at Adriana.  She shrugged her shoulders. His brow creased, as he watched his mother playing with Tyler's tiny hand.

April carried the baby over and placed him in Hayden's arms. He took him rather awkwardly. April gave a small laugh, which surprised them all. "He won't break, you know."

Hayden frowned, "He's so little. I'm scared I might hurt him."

"He's a Radcliff, son. We're a tough lot, we Radcliff's." She moved in and gave him an awkward hug "I'm happy for you Hayden," She glanced over at Adriana. "You made an excellent choice and I wish you both the best." April walked over to the bed and kissed Adriana on the cheek. "I must be going Congratulations my dear, and thank you."

"Nanny," Madison cried as she reached across to give April a hug, nearly flooring Hayden.

April wrapped her arms around her granddaughter and kissed her on the cheek. "So Madison, what do you think of your new baby brother?"

Madison's nose wrinkled, "He looks yucky. Mommy said he will look better soon."

April smiled at Adriana, "Well Mommy's right. It won't be long before you can help to look after him and teach him things."

"I'm going to draw him a picture."

"Are you just? I think he would like that. Well, goodbye Sweetheart. Now you be good for Mommy and Daddy. I'll see you soon."

Hayden stood staring at the door long after his Mother had left. He turned to Adriana, "What had just happened here? That wasn't my mother."

Adriana smiled, "Let's just say with a bit of perseverance I managed to mend a few broken fences."

"Why? I thought we had decided it was best to keep our distance?"

"I couldn't stand the thought of your mother being shut out of your life, no matter how much she deserved it. I could see it was hurting you."

"I won't have her bullying you. You have enough to do with a new baby."

"Honestly Hayden, its fine. Your mother and I have come to an understanding. I think she actually likes me now, in her own abrupt selfish way. And believe it or not Madison adores her."

"So why didn't you tell me?"

"I wanted it to be a surprise. In the beginning I wasn't sure it was going to work"

He smiled, "Well it was certainly a surprise." He looked across at his sister, "did you know about this?"

"Well, sort of."

"Sort of. What does that  mean?"


There was a soft tap at the door. Hayden turned to see Brian standing there, clutching a small velvet box in his hand. Adriana's face broke into a smile.

"Brian, come here and give me a hug and take a look at your new grandson."

He strode over to the bed, handing Hayden the box as he passed. He peeked in at the sleeping baby, now cradled in Adriana's arms.

"He's going to break a few hearts, that one."

Adriana frowned, "No he's not. He's going to find a beautiful intelligent, sexy woman and settle down and have a family."

They all laughed,

"What? What's wrong with that?"

Brian stepped away as Hayden walked up to the bed. He sat on the edge of the bed and took the ring out of the box. Adriana gasped, her hand flew to her mouth and tears began to well in her eyes. He gazed at her, his eyes moist.

"Adriana, this may not be the most romantic of places to do this but I couldn't bear to wait a minute longer. You are the most beautiful woman I have ever met. You loved me even though I felt I had nothing to give. You let me become part of your family and showed me how to love unconditionally. And now you have given me a son," he glanced over at Madi "and a daughter. Adriana would you please do me the honour of becoming my wife?"

Her jaw dropped open as tears flooded her cheeks.

"Yes, yes... a thousand times yes."

Hayden stood up and slipped the ring on her finger, then sat down on the bed beside her. Madison climbed onto his knee. The baby lay cradled in the crook of Adriana's arm. Hayden smiled down at his family. He now had everything a man could want. His mother's surprise visit had been totally unexpected. It was still hard to believe that his mother actually liked his future wife. That was certainly one for the record books. He had never heard her utter anything even close to an apology. Admitting that he had made the right choice was probably  the closest thing he would get. He placed a kiss on his fiancé's forehead. The others came over to congratulate them. Brian shook Hayden's hand.

"Thanks for picking up the ring."

"Don't give it another thought."

Adriana looked up at Brian, "You knew about this?"

He smiled, "Yes."

Adriana looked up at Hayden, "Do you think this is a good start? Keeping secrets from each other?"

He smiled, "Some secrets are worth keeping. Anyway what about the mother thing? Wasn't that a secret?"

"No, I classify that under damage control."

"I suppose I'll let you have that one, but only because I love you."

"You know, that's the first time you've actually said that you love me."

He grinned, "Old habits die hard, but I promise I'm a quick learner."

She reached up and pulled him close, "I love you too."

Madi pushed between them, "I love everybody too," she wrinkled her nose, as she looked down at Tyler, "even him."

They all laughed.

# Chapter Twenty Six

Adriana looked across at Hayden sprawled uncomfortably in the chair. "Hayden... Hayden."
 His eyes opened slowly as he sat up and rubbed his neck. "Why don't you go home for a bit and get some sleep?" He rose to his feet and walked over to her. "I can't bear to be away from you, not even for a second."
"Well if you don't get some sleep soon, you are going to crash. We are fine now, go and get some rest."
"If you're sure."
"I'm sure. Tyler is sleeping. I might try and catch a few minute's sleep while he's out."
"I'll call back later. Do you want me to bring anything?"
She smiled, "Just a fresher, cleaner you."
He bowed, "Your wish is my command."
"Sounds intriguing."

"Enough of your flirting, woman."

He grinned, "New rule, no teasing until you are ready for action."

"Six weeks. Do you think you can last that long?"

"For you my dear, anything is possible."

She giggled, "I will see you later then."

With a quick kiss and he was gone. She gave a long sigh and rested her head back against the pillow. The door opened, she blinked sleepily, expecting it to be Hayden saying that he had forgotten something.

He hesitated at the door. "I'm sorry, I didn't know you were sleeping. I could come back later."

"Ross! Don't you dare. Come in."

"I met Hayden in the foyer." He held out a bunch of flowers. "I was just going to drop these at the desk for you but Hayden insisted I come and see you."

"He did?"

"It surprised me a little to. If you're not comfortable with me being here, I can go."

She patted the bed beside her, "Come and sit with me." Placing the flowers on the bench he walked over and perched himself on the edge of bed.

"How have things been, with the store?"

"Great... I do miss our little chats though."

"Me too, I've been going crazy with no one to talk to about things."

He smiled, "Really?"

She nodded, "Come here and give me a hug."

He wrapped his arms around her. "Congratulations, by the way." He pulled  back, "I'm sorry for being such an idiot."

"You weren't, honestly don't worry about it. It's all in the past."

 He glanced at the ring on her finger. "So he asked you to marry him then?"

"Yep, isn't it great?"

Ross picked up her hand and studied the ring. "Yeah great. This must have cost him a small fortune."

"Ross."

"I'm sorry. I didn't mean it the way it sounded. I'm happy for you, honestly."

"So, friends again?"

He nodded. "But don't think you're getting any more freebies." He tried to hide his smile, "Not with a rock like that on your finger."

She laughed, "Deal. I won't be back at the store for a bit though. But that doesn't mean I can't pop in to see you, once in a while."

His eyes met hers, "I'd be hurt if you didn't, but make sure you bring Madi with you and the baby." Ross glanced over at the crib. "Can I have a look?"

"By all means, just don't wake him." He crept over and peeked into the crib.

"They aren't the prettiest things, are they?"

"Neither would you be if you'd been cramped up and floating in liquid for the past nine months."

"True. He has blonde hair."

"And."

"Just an observation."

He turned to look at her. "You deserve this. You and he are so right for each other. I've seen the way he looks at you. He loves you deeply."

"I know.  I never thought I would ever feel happy again."

"I glad you have finally found happiness. That's all I ever wanted for you."

"I know and thank you. It's nice to know you are there when I need you. As perfect as Hayden seems I know there will be times when I need a friend."

"Whenever you need me, you only need ask. Well, I had better be going. As much as I agree with your choice of man, I'm still not quite ready to chat with him."

"I can understand that. Come here and give me one last hug before you go." He walked over and wrapped his arms around her. "Congratulations Adriana. By the way when is the wedding?

"I have no idea. You will receive an invitation."

"I'll look forward to it. Well goodbye, and pop in soon for a chat."

"I will, goodbye." She watched him leave. A smile touched her lips, now she could honestly say everything was perfect.


A little while later Tyler began to cry. She threw back the covers and reached over to pick him up. Dropping her gown off her shoulder, she placed him at the breast. Hayden entered at that precise moment. He smiled, "I've never seen anything more beautiful."

"That is debatable, I haven't showered,  my  hair's  a

mess and I have a lot of trouble sitting down; and I think your son has just filled his nappy.”

He laughed, “Besides all that.” He sat down on the side of the bed and stroked his son’s head. “He’s certainly latched onto the breast feeding thing pretty quickly.”

She grinned, “He's a quick learner, just like his father.”

“Did Ross come and see you?”

“Yes he did, thank you for insisting he come.”

“To be honest, at first I didn’t really want him anywhere near you. I realised he means a lot to you and I’m not about to start dictating to you who you can and can’t see. As long as you don’t run off on holiday with him again, I’m sure I can tolerate him.”

“Thank you, I’m sorry to say the same can’t be said for Jessica. If I catch her anywhere near you, there will be hell to pay.”

“Don’t you trust me?”

“Oh I trust you all right, it’s her I don’t.”

He leant forward and kissed her forehead, “Well rumour has it that she is leaving town. She has found some other poor unsuspecting man to lay her affections on. She knows when she is beaten.”

“I’ve been thinking. Why don’t we introduce Janice to Ross?”

“What!”

“She’s single, he’s a nice guy. You never know.”

“You just concentrate on being a mother and leave the match making well alone.”

“They would make a cute couple, don’t you think?”

“No I don’t, now promise me you’ll leave it alone.”

"I'm promising no such thing."

"Adriana I'm warning you, don't meddle. If it's meant to be it will happen."

"How? It's not as if she goes down town for an ice cream, is it." A smile played on her lips as a thought occurred to her.

"You can wipe that smile off your face. I mean it Adriana, you leave it alone."

She gave an exasperated sigh, "fine, if they meet they meet."

He eyed her suspiciously. "I'm not sure I can trust you."

"Look I promise, I won't introduce them. Are you happy with that?"

Yes. I don't believe in match making."

"So you said. I've promised, what more do you want?"

"I suppose I'll have to trust you, won't I?"

# Chapter Twenty Seven

Madison skipped along the street beside Janice. "There it is," she said, pointing across the street. Janice gripped Madison's hand tightly as they crossed the street. Once they were safely on the other side, Madison slipped her hand free and ran up the pavement.

"Madison, wait." Janice hurried after her.

Madison pushed open the store door and ran inside.

"Madi! Hello my baby girl." Ross said as he lifted her in the air and swung her around. "What brings you down here, are you with Mommy?"

He looked toward the door as the bell jingled. He stopped and stood staring as the blonde beauty entered the store.

She glanced at Madison perched in his arms. Her brow creased, "I don't think that is at all appropriate, do you?"

"What, this?" he replied, jiggling Madison in his arms. She gave a soft little giggle.

"I'm sorry, but I'm going to have to ask you to put her down."

"Come on, lady. I've known her since she was in nappies."

"The name is Janice. And while Adriana is not present I would feel more comfortable if Madison was standing on her own two feet."

Ross placed Madison down on the floor. His eyes turned to the woman. "I don't really appreciate you hinting that there is something sordid about me holding her."

Her pale blue eyes met his with a steely determination. "Well, that is just too bad. As I said, while I am responsible for her I would appreciate it if you kept your hands to yourself."

"Who did you say you were again?"

Janice Radcliff. Hayden's sister."

"Oh.. that explains it all."

Her soft pink painted lips pouted slightly, "Excuse me?"

"Nothing." His eyes took in her long slender form. The pencil skirt she wore hugged her body, accentuating the slight roundness to her hips and the long length of thighs. He drew his eyes away. There certainly wasn't much point in having a body as fine as hers if there was no warmth inside. Adriana may find the whole Radcliff family intriguing but he certainly didn't.

"So what will it be, Madi?"'

Madison walked along the counter, pointing to the various flavours.

Janice shifted nervously as she watched his dark hair fall across his forehead. He gave a quick glance up and caught her watching him. He gave her a forced smile, which she returned with equal discomfort.

The ice cream's on the house by the way."

"I couldn't possibly."

"You don't have any choice. Would  you care for an ice cream?" He asked looking right at her.

She hadn't noticed before, but his eyes were a deep golden brown. They were kind eyes.

He gave her a genuine smile and she found herself smiling back.

"No, I'm fine thank you."

"Let me guess. You're watching your waistline."

Her eyes narrowed.

"It's certainly doesn't look like it needs watching. Indulge yourself once in a while, why don't you?"

"I indulge myself plenty, thank you very much. Now how much do I owe you?"

He gave a sigh, "It's on the house. You know, a woman who can't indulge in a little ice cream once in a while is a sad woman indeed."

"Excuse me."

"You heard."

"For your information, I do eat ice cream."

"Sure you do."

"Listen here. I don't appreciate being judged."

"I'm not judging you. It's just an observation that's all."

She stood staring at him defiantly. "Fine, just to prove a point I'll have a double chocolate ripple."

His eyebrows rose. "Very daring for a first timer."

Her eyes narrowed. "Just give me the damn ice cream."

He quickly made it up and handed it to her.

She looked at it as though it was going to instantly turn her into a big lump of Jell-O.

He laughed, "You've never had one, have you?"

"Of course I have, you silly man."

"Go on then, give it a good lick."

"I'm not here for your entertainment."

"I knew you wouldn't."

Fixing her eyes on his, she took a long slow lick around the tip of ice cream.

He felt movement in his groin region.

A smile hinted at the corner of her lips, "There, you satisfied now?"

His eyes widened.

She turned on her heel, "Come on, let's go. Good day to you..."

"The name's Ross."

"Ross." She hissed through gritted teeth.

Grabbing Madison's hand she stormed from the store tossing the ice cream in the bin as she passed. Ross stood shaking his head as he  watched them disappear down the street.

# Chapter Twenty Eight

Adriana struggled out of the car as Hayden made his way to the house carrying the baby and several bags. Adriana gingerly walked the path, carrying one of the bags and her cushion which she never went without. He turned to smile at her. "Welcome home", he opened the door and held it open whilst she walked through. A high pitched yapping sounded from the sunroom. She glanced across at him. Madison came running down the hall.

"Madison wait, no jumping." Adriana cried.

Madison pulled to a sudden stop in front of her. "I know. Daddy already told me."

Next minute a golden ball of energy came bounding down the hall and crashed into the back of Madison's knees, she was thrown forward and landed heavily against the unsuspecting Adriana. She felt herself falling and quickly tossed her cushion behind her. She gritted her teeth, pain tearing through her abdomen as she landed heavily on her cushion. The puppy launched itself on top of her, licking her face furiously. She began to laugh much to Hayden's relief.

"Madi, I asked you to keep the puppy in its pen."

"Sorry, that was me." said Janice walking up the passage toward them. "I didn't realise he would cause such mayhem."

Hayden handed her the baby as he helped Adriana to her feet. "Are you okay?"

"I'm fine, I'm not made of china."

He smiled, Sorry, it wasn't quite the homecoming I had envisaged."

Her eyes met his, "Any home coming is  good, no matter what happens. So  does  this little dynamo have a name?"

"His name is Jake," said Madi excitedly. He does wee's on the floor."

Adriana smiled, as she glanced over at Hayden "Oh does he now?"

Hayden shrugged, "House training has a way to go."

"Well I vote you in as chief instructor and wee cleaner. I have baby nappies to deal with, so the dog I'm afraid is your domain."

"I'll help," squealed Madi, "but not the wee stuff."

They all laughed as they made their way through to the living room.

"Janice can you just watch the baby for a minute? I have something I want to show Adriana."

Janice winked at him, "Sure, no problem. But if he cries

you will have to come running."

"He's just had a feed, so he should be fine for a while." Hayden took her by the hand and led her upstairs.

Her brow creased when they reached the bedroom door. "You do realize I'm not up for any funny business, right?" He looked slightly offended but said nothing. He took her hand and lead her into the room. She glanced about; everything seemed the same. She looked at him questioningly. He led her over to the side of the room. Her brow rose when she suddenly realised there was a door that hadn't been there before. He turned the handle and pushed it open. She let out a delighted gasp. He had set up a nursery. All done in soft blues and white with clever splashes of colour around the room with a bright lemon rocking chair, a bookshelf filled with books and a cheerful mobile hanging above the beautifully carved wooden crib. "It's wonderful", she threw her arms around him. "so this was my surprise?"

He smiled "So, do you like it?"

"Like it? I love it."

"I designed it so that later on when we are finished with the whole baby making thing, you can turn it into a dressing room or study or something." He guided her over to the window.

Tears welled in her eyes, "It looks over the spot where he was conceived. I hope you're not suggesting that all our children are to be conceived there?"

"No of course not, but it wouldn't hurt testing it out once in a while."

Janice entered the room carrying Tyler, "So, what do you

think?"
Adriana's cheeks heated a little, but Janice showed no sign of having heard any of their conversation." I thought it might be best if you put him to sleep up here, what with all the noise Madi and the puppy are making. I was expecting him to wake up any minute". Adriana took him from her and placed him into the crib.
"He looks so little in there. Before we know it he'll be running around the yard with Madi and I'll be expecting another."
Hayden's eyebrows rose. "Steady on, I'm still getting used to the two I have, I wasn't serious about a rugby team. You do know that right?"
"I'm just teasing, two ,three even four, I don't care which as long as I'm with you."
Janice gave a long sigh "Okay, as usual that's my cue to leave. I was thinking of taking Madi and the puppy down onto the beach to give you both a little time together. How does that sound?"
 Relief showed in Adriana's face. "Would you, that would be great, thanks."
Janice turned to leave, "I'm really happy for you both."
"Thanks Sis. Now beat it."
"Hayden, that's not very brotherly."
"What can I say?  I've missed having you in my arms."
They stood at the window and watched Janice, Madison and the puppy make their way down onto the beach.
She snuggled back against him, "I still can't believe that one chance meeting on the beach lead to all this."
He kissed the side of her neck, neither can I."